To Ken
♡ Mi

MW01079155

PRINCESS THE CAT
DEFEATS THE EMPEROR

A CAT AND DOG CHILDREN'S BOOK
CHRISTMAS CAPER

JOHN HEATON

FLANNEL AND FLASHLIGHT PRESS

Join the Flannel and Flashlight Newsletter for a FREE ebook.

Only subscribers like you will discover Princess' full story.

http://bit.ly/FandFNewsletter

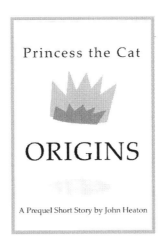

1

The oldest girl child unloads another massive scoop of Thanksgiving mashed potatoes onto her plate, and the big woman person declares to everybody else around the dinner table, "Your father had better not get another Charlie Brown Christmas tree this year."

The big man person chews his turkey, probably planning how he will discover the perfect Christmas tree this winter.

Meow?

Max, the other cat I allow in my house, is begging like a dog for a few scraps of Thanksgiving dinner. I don't deny that I look forward to turkey and stuffing later, but I need to leave for a rendezvous with a spy.

I pass through my eating room and into my garage, and then I exit the door on the side of my garage into my front yard. My gray tabby fur bristles from the cold that descends upon my domain as I trot down Rover Boulevard towards Grand Canyon Drive. I have a secret meeting with a cat who rules a small domain along Grand Canyon Drive. He is my spy, and I only call him by his codename: *Mozart*.

I have not even told the Cat Council about *Mozart* to keep him safe, especially from the evil Emperor who threatens my territory.

The Emperor had been, for years, only a vague threat, somewhere in the far east of my town. More recently, I have received messages that he has been aggressively expanding his territory. Some animals have fled west as refugees, bringing tales of terror of what a cruel tyrant the Emperor is. Other than that, I know nothing about this Emperor.

I reach a tree on Grand Canyon Drive without incident. All the people in houses as I pass by are feasting on a Thanksgiving meal, the children anxiously plotting what they will implore from Santa Claus, and all the animals look forward to growing fat off the people's excess food, especially the turkey.

I wait in the tree along Grand Canyon Drive for *Mozart*, but his tardiness distresses me.

He is never late like this. I hope he just got distracted by the new holiday season.

Weeks ago, *Mozart* contacted me through Jacques, a freedom fighter cat who, along with his band of resistance fighters, lives in the junkyard. I've never met Jacques. He only communicates with me through messengers. Jacques makes it his business to know what is going on all over the town of White Rock and to make sure that there is freedom for pets and animals everywhere. So far, this Jacques has not impeded the rule of my domain. He may be a useful ally against the Emperor. Jacques made it seem urgent for me to meet the cat I now call *Mozart*. Our first meeting was as disappointing as lite cat food. *Mozart* revealed nothing, other than the fact that he was afraid of something.

Maybe whatever he was afraid of has caused him to be late for this meeting.

Or worse.

The silence of the night is broken by the roar of a large vehicle and screeching tires racing towards my hiding spot. My ears twitch and my eyes zoom in to see what it is. I fear a truck has run over *Mozart*, but that's not the case.

Fierce dog barks and growls erupt along with the roaring engine and screeching tires, and then the vehicle stops. I can't see the dog, but I can see the large van clearly.

Animal Control is written on the side of the vehicle. Three surly men in uniforms get out of the van carrying various weaponry to wield against the monstrous dog.

The men assault the dog, yelling, and even using words my children people are not allowed to use, as the barking and growling continues from this beastly dog that I have not yet been able to see.

The conflagration lasts for minutes—*nobody can withstand Animal Control that long!*—but the three Animal Control workers wrestle what must be a monstrous dog in a net into the back of the van. Afterward, the Animal Control workers limp and clasp their bodily injuries while they grumble to themselves.

"I can't believe that dog," one of them says. "Talk about ruining my Thanksgiving."

"That dog is some kind of monster," another Animal Control worker agrees.

The Animal Control van drives away, and I'm thankful they did not spot me. I am not at home, I don't have a collar or tags so as to not attract coyotes, and I certainly did not want to be put in the back of the Animal Control van with whatever that dog was they just captured, even if he is caged.

I wait a few more moments for *Mozart*, but he never shows up. That monster dog and Animal Control plus *Mozart's* disappearance can't be a coincidence. This region of town has been changing for the worse, and I get the feeling that an invisible Iron Curtain has descended upon Grand Canyon Drive, dividing the town in half. I shudder to think what may soon threaten my domain from beyond Grand Canyon Drive, this Wall creating two different worlds. I'm certain the Emperor is responsible.

I go back home warily. I can hear Chief in his pen sloppily chowing down what must be leftover turkey and stuffing. Chief is the big friendly old dog who lives next door, one of my loyal subjects and a key adviser. I decide not to say anything to Chief at this point.

There's no point in ruining this holiday by sharing a threat that I only have a gut feeling about.

Animal Control captured that monster dog, and Mozart may have just been late, I reassure myself.

I reenter my house, and I find Max in my eating room also eating leftover Thanksgiving turkey.

To my people's credit, I notice that they left me more Thanksgiving food than Max. I don't say anything to Max about *Mozart*, either.

"Why can't I go Black Friday shopping tomorrow?" the oldest girl child demands of her parents in the other room.

"I already told you why, and I'm not going to discuss it anymore," the big man person replies impatiently.

"You never let me do anything fun," she complains. "Can I

have a sleepover, then?"

"Not this weekend," the big man person says. "How about during Christmas break?"

This response placates the oldest girl child. She doesn't reply.

The Thanksgiving feast just doesn't taste the same with the trouble looming over my domain. I fear for *Mozart's* life. Perhaps his apprehension during our first meeting was justified. And even though Animal Control captured that menacing dog, I fear a plot from the Emperor.

What if that dog were to escape from Animal Control?

"Once you're done eating," I tell Max, "inform Tweedledee and Tweedledum about our next Cat Council meeting. It will be at the usual place, under the lilac bush, and the usual time."

"Yes, ma'am," Max replies in between bites.

I watch Max leave after he's done eating to go inform Tweedledee and Tweedledum about the Cat Council meeting, and I mull over all the possibilities as I inhale not only turkey, but the most delicious sausage stuffing I have ever eaten—at least since last year, anyways.

IT IS time for my monthly Cat Council meeting, the first Tuesday of December. This is something new I instituted to ensure that all of us cats are allied and understand that I am in charge. The four of us-that is, Max, the twins, Tweedledee and Tweedledum, and I-gather behind a lilac bush in the backyard of my house. I make sure that we are not in a circle. We are not equals, and I am not the first among equals. I face the three of them as their leader, as the empress over my domain.

"Now that you have all stated your pledge of allegiance to me, your empress," I say, "does anybody remember what the first item on the agenda is?"

Three paws shoot up into the air.

These three younger cats are excited that I include them in running my domain. The twins practically bounce up and down, raising their paws in the air. Max lunges to raise his paw higher than the other two. I sigh at this childish behavior.

I call on Max.

"We need to discuss the new people moving into the empty neighbor's house," Max says. The twins give Max a sidelong glance, jealous that I called on him. Tweedledum, the boy twin kitten, raises his paw.

"Yes?" I say.

"As instructed," Tweedledum says with a sharp look at Max, "Tweedledee and I gathered intelligence about this new family who will move in."

"Excellent. Report."

"They move in this week," Tweedledee says. The now vacant house is the same house that had a possum trap in my earlier adventures. It is also where the rattlesnake temporarily lived. You never know what kind of troublemakers might inhabit a vacant house.

"These people are moving from a house beyond Grand Canyon Drive," Tweedledum adds.

My eyes narrow.

"We think they have children, but we have not been able to ascertain what kind or how many," Tweedledee says.

"But," Tweedledum says, "we do know one enticing thing." Tweedledum looks at us to draw us in for his juicy gossip. "They have a pet."

"What kind?" I demand.

"It is a parrot. A talking bird," Tweedledum answers.

"So what?" I say. "Even Max can talk. No offense, Max."

"But this parrot can talk like a person, and it can also talk like an animal," Tweedledee says.

"What do you mean?" I ask.

"Yeah," Max butts in. "What do you mean?"

"We mean," Tweedledum says, "that this talking bird can talk to you and me just like any other animal. However, this talking bird can also talk with humans using people words and people language."

Tweedledee and Tweedledum sit up proudly and puff their chests out.

"That is a power I am deeply suspicious of," I say. "Unprecedented. What sort of beast can bridge the gap between devolved humans and civilized cats?"

"*I know. I know,*" Max says, thrusting his paw up in the air.

"It's a rhetorical question," I say. "If a cat like me can't do it, then what does that say about this bird?" I look at the three other cats on the Cat Council, but they keep their paws down from fear of a scolding.

"This is new territory," I warn. "We must be cautious of this flying beast. The fact that this family comes from beyond Grand Canyon Drive is also suspicious. Is it a coincidence that they are coming from the Emperor's Evil Empire?"

Max raises his paw halfway before my glare forces him to lower it. Tweedledum mouths the words, "Rhetorical question," to Max in rebuke.

"When this family moves in," I say, "we need to send patrols into their yard. These will serve two main purposes. First, they will be a means of gathering intelligence on these spies, enemies of my empire. We must discover how many children they have. What if they have a child like Todd?"

The three shudder at the mention of the incorrigible teenage boy in town who has a penchant for tormenting animals.

"Secondly," I continue, "we need to acclimate this new family to our presence. If we constantly move in and out of their yard from the first day they move in, then they won't suspect anything later when they continue to see cats. Understood?"

Three cat heads nod in response.

"That brings us to the next item on our agenda," I say as I notice snowflakes beginning to fall gently from the sky. "This rival who calls himself 'The Emperor,' recently expanded his domain as far as Grand Canyon Drive. A family that is moving out of his kingdom into mine? I suspect this family is being sent to spy on me." The three other cats on the Council have their eyes wide open, perhaps realizing that Grand Canyon Drive is only about ten minutes away.

"In addition," I say, "a messenger—an emissary—from the Emperor is joining us for part of this meeting. Tweedledum, go fetch the messenger from this Emperor." I can't resist rolling my eyes as I say, "Emperor."

When the emissary joins us, snow has accumulated on his back. He is not at all what I expected.

THE EMISSARY of the Emperor waddles into our presence. I expected a bit more *gravitas*. Instead, he is a Max look-alike, complete with long orange fur and white feet. He jangles into my presence. I can't hold back a scowl when I see and hear a collar with a bell around his neck. Another detail pushes this emissary beyond the edge of goofy: he is wearing a cat sweater as if he were a dog. It is green and red, with white snowflakes knitted into it. Does he not realize that one of our points of superiority is our fur that allows us to self-groom? Cats don't need clothes, and we don't need special rooms and hoses to wash ourselves like people.

"Wow," Max gasps. "My long-lost twin."

The emissary ignores Max, and instead proceeds to say: "I am the emissary of the Mighty Emperor, vanquisher of coyotes—"

Only because I defeated Snarl first, I think to myself.

But he continues, "—and said Emperor has expanded his domain in these recent days to extend peace, prosperity, and stability as far as even Grand Canyon Drive.

"The Emperor expects cooperation with his empire so that peace and prosperity may spread to more and more animals, especially cats."

He pauses, and I look at the Cat Council. Max and the twins are confused by his bizarre appearance and his surprisingly commanding speech. I sigh as I pick at my claws. Otherwise, he would think I care about what he has to say. The emissary drones on.

"The Emperor shares his condolences over the death of the previous ruler of Grand Canyon Drive. It was an unfortunate death." He pauses slightly when he says, "Unfortunate." *Mozart* was the previous ruler over Grand Canyon Drive, and this makes me certain that the Emperor is responsible for the disappearance of *Mozart*.

"I bring a letter from the Emperor, but it is more than a

letter," the emissary says. "It is an opportunity. In this letter are the terms of cooperating with his empire." The emissary lays down a piece of parchment paper amid the Cat Council. I read it in seconds.

Max and the twins ask: "What does this mean, Princess?" I don't answer them.

"Enjoy your journey back to the Emperor," I say. I hold the gaze of the emissary, and after a few seconds he turns around and jingles away.

The Emperor's terms of cooperation require that I pay the Emperor tribute. He will have regular inspections of my domain. He will have permanent advisers and counselors to ensure that peace, prosperity, and his will flourish in my domain. All for our good, of course. This Emperor is making a mistake. I am Princess, the empress of my domain, and I do not share my authority with any other.

"What a goofball," Tweedledee says after the emissary is gone. "What kind of fashion sense does this Emperor have?"

"And that collar with the bell," Tweedledum says. "Doesn't he know it attracts coyotes?"

"Maybe he's confident his Emperor has vanquished coyotes," Max suggests. "We don't need to worry about this goofy Emperor at all."

"Don't trust the Emperor," I say. "Certainly don't trust his emissaries, regardless of how goofy they appear. Be on the lookout, especially during these holidays. 'Christmas is a time for secrets,' my people always say."

Max and the twins exchange wary glances, and I wonder if they are confused, or if they have their own secrets.

"That brings us to the third and final item on the agenda," I say. "Rules for the holidays."

"CAN I tell them the holiday rules?" Max says. He raises his paw in the air as if he's trying to touch the top of the lilac bush even though his eyes are still locked on me.

"Go ahead," I concede.

Max does an adequate job of stating all the holiday rules, but I do have to correct him about not chewing the wires of Christmas lights.

"You sure?" Max asks. "They seem so enticing."

"That's exactly why I make it a point to tell you not to chew on them," I say. "It would electrocute you."

"That's ... bad?" Max asks.

"It would definitely be shocking."

"Okay," Tweedledum says. "We will not chew on any Christmas lights."

"I did remember some additional rules you all need to know," I say.

"More rules?" Tweedledee asks. "Aren't holidays supposed to be fun?"

"The rules are for your own good," I remind her. "Be kind to groups of people who enter my domain and sing songs at people's doorsteps. Eat all the extra holiday food, but don't choke on bones. Don't drink the thick beverage they call eggnog; it's not milk. Again, I must emphasize: do not climb Christmas trees.

"Last, but not least," I continue, "be on the lookout for any suspicious characters. I sense the Emperor, as he fancies himself, is up to something sinister. If there are any problems, I will call an emergency Cat Council meeting."

"We'll be there," Max says proudly.

"As for the Emperor's conditions for cooperation," I say as I crouch over the paper, "here's what I think of them."

I go pee on the piece of paper.

"*Ahhhh.* Council adjourned."

I watch the three other cats walk away from our Council meeting, but when I look at the paper I just peed on, I notice something unusual.

THE MOIST, and now steaming, paper reveals more writing coming into focus. The wet portions of the paper are more translucent, and the new writing is slightly more opaque. I can make out the words, "helping you but," but the rest is illegible.

The snow falls harder now, and I want to go inside, but this mysterious writing has my interest. I peek around my yard to make sure that nobody else is watching. I squat over the paper again, and I soak it in urine.

As if by magic, more writing appears on the paper. The words come into focus. It reads, "I will help you, but then I want out." Another sentence appears, "Look for empty cat food cans."

I stare at the piece of paper for a few minutes, not sure what to make of it, or what to do about it. Surely this message is not from the emissary himself. Who is willing to help me? And who wants out? If they had access to this message, they must be close to the Emperor. I certainly don't need their help, but they have gotten my attention like a laser pointer. I cover the message with dirt and bury it.

I walk over to Chief's pen. He is the only adviser I trust. The snow falls heavily now, even building up on my back, but I need to speak with Chief. I call out to him from the fence that overlooks his pen.

"I've got a brainteaser for you, Chief," I call out. I don't see Chief, but I know he's hiding from the snow in his doghouse. He sticks his head out slightly so that snowflakes land on his nose.

"Who says my brain wants to be teased, anyhow?" Chief asks.

"I just had a meeting with the Cat Council. Sorry you couldn't be included, by the way, but my real reason for the Council isn't to rule my domain."

"What is your real reason?" Chief asks.

"You know what they say, don't you?" I ask. "*Keep your friends close, and your enemies closer.*"

"Sounds like something from a movie to me," Chief observes, "and I'm wondering who on the Cat Council is considered your enemy. What kind of life do you have if you can't trust those closest to you?"

"Max has saved my life," I say, "and so he is definitely my friend. Those twin kittens, however, are the ones I suspect."

"Where do I fit in?" Chief asks.

"You're a dog," I say. "You can't be on the Cat Council."

"Before my nose freezes off," Chief says, "what is this brainteaser?"

I give Chief a brief update as to all that transpired at the Cat Council. To tell him about the secret message, I hop down off the fence and into his pen. I walk over to his doghouse, and Chief draws his nose back in.

"You never come into my pen," Chief says.

"I can't risk anybody else hearing this," I say. "I don't care if I'm in a dog's pen, so listen carefully."

I whisper to Chief the details of the letter. To my satisfaction, I see a faint glimmer in his eyes and a smile creep across his face.

"Whoever wrote that message is using some exciting spy tactics," Chief says. "It's old-fashioned, invisible ink, as old as the spying profession itself."

"What do you know about spying?" I say. "An old dog like you can't find anything. Cats are the best spies."

"Do you want my help, or do you just want to insult me?" Chief says.

"Sorry," I say, "but I couldn't resist. Carry on." My fake apology is sufficient, and so Chief continues.

"In spy movies and TV shows, there are people who spy for the other side. The spy secretly works inside an organization or government for the bad guys, and he is called a mole. It's like they hide underground, and they sneak out information to the other side, for example. The mole could be a high-ranking spy in a government. From a high position in government, he could leak secret military plans to the other side. This could help the other side, but the mole has to keep his identity secret so that he can continue to help the other side."

"Cunning, and yet traitorous," I say.

"Traitorous, indeed," Chief says. "Spies and moles get in big trouble when caught."

"So, the Emperor has a mole," I say, more to myself than to Chief.

"Exactly."

"Who could the mole be?" I ask. "Could it be the emissary? Could it be somebody else that I don't even know yet?"

"At this point, you should continue communication with the Emperor," Chief advises. "That will give the mole more opportunity to communicate with you. Look out for empty cans of cat food that may contain a message. Hopefully, you could establish some sort of consistent way to communicate back and forth with this mole."

"Excellent idea," I say to Chief. After a few seconds, I say, "I'm glad I thought of it." I make my way to the fence and hop on top of it to go home.

As I make one more lap around my domain before I go into my garage to warm up on top of those large portable heaters my people call cars, I notice something odd about one of the nearby houses. It is the house diagonally behind my house, the same one that new people will soon move into from Grand Canyon Drive.

From on top of the fence, I see cat tracks in the fresh snow, tracks that are being covered by the still falling snow. Since the snow started falling during the Cat Council meeting, the tracks must have been left after the Council meeting. I look around, but I don't see anybody else. I move closer to the tracks in the front yard of the empty house, and I now see two sets of tracks.

One set of tracks leads back into my domain before it ends at a fence. My eyes follow the other set of tracks into the distance. They could eventually lead anywhere. My body stiffens as I ponder the fact that, at least as far as I can see, the tracks head towards Grand Canyon Drive, the Emperor's new territory. I know that Max does not enjoy walking on fences, and I know that the twins, Tweedledee and Tweedledum, are the only other cats in my domain. One, or both of those twins, is working against me, and meeting with somebody who works for the Emperor.

The Emperor has a mole, but I fear that I have a mole as well.

2

The snow falls heavily this night, so I spend it in my garage. Max does the same, but he wakes me up from my nap on top of the car early in the morning.

"Something's wrong," Max says as he nudges me awake. "The big man person has usually driven away with this car by now." Normally, waking me up from sleep would draw a sharp rebuke, but Max has a point. I hop down and stick my head out the cat door that leads outside the garage. I see something I've not seen in years. Pure white snow, undisturbed, blankets everything as far as I can see.

"What?" Max asks. "Did something happen?"

As if to answer Max's question, the youngest girl child yells inside the house: "Snow day! No school! Snow day!"

So that's why the big man person hasn't left for work. Work and school are canceled. Max follows me as I enter the house. The youngest girl child is gazing out a window at the winter wonderland. The middle boy child is up as well, and he only has one thing to say when he sees the snow.

"There's going to be a snowball fight."

The big man person listens to the radio as usual, but it sounds different this morning. Instead of old music, the voice announces school delays and cancellations.

"Let's wake Sarah up to play in the snow," the youngest girl child says to her brother. She and her older brother tromp to her bedroom, but they return moments later, disappointed.

"How come all she wants to do is sleep?" the youngest girl child asks.

"Makes sense, except on a snow day," the middle boy child says.

The youngest girl child and the middle boy child do something I've never seen them do. Faster than me on a hot tin roof, they eat breakfast, put on their clothes, and then put on snow pants, winter jackets, fluffy hats, snow boots, and mittens and gloves. They join the other neighborhood children who, with a strange sense of choreography, pour out of their houses and onto the virgin white snow in their yards.

I decide to watch all the children play in the snow from up in the willow tree. Over the next hour, a chain of snow forts, walls, tunnels, and pathways connect my yard with several of our neighbors' yards. It's amazing the amount of work all those children get done when they're interested and motivated to build something of their own.

Even Chief, as old as he is, can't contain his excitement about the snow. He's out of his pen, moving with a speed and grace that I did not think possible. He spots me up in the tree.

"The cold soothes my aching bones," Chief says, as if he needs an excuse.

"Capture the flag snowball fight!" rings out amongst the children. The children divide into two teams. One team gathers in the now vacant yard diagonally behind my back yard. This is the house and yard the new neighbors will be moving into. The other team gathers in the backyard that shares Chief's pen. My people's children are on the team with Chief's pen.

The rules of the game are simple. The teams have thirty minutes to make snowballs, build snow forts, and hide their red flag anywhere in their territory. Players invade the other team's territory, and their goal is to find the flag, steal it, and bring it back to their own home base without getting hit by a snowball. If a player is hit by a snowball, then they have to return to their own territory. Once a player is hit with a snowball three times, then they have to sit in "jail" for five minutes. If all the players on one team are in jail at once, then the other team wins. Other than that, the team to grab the flag and bring it back to their own base is the winner.

What I observe is far more exciting than any football, basketball, or baseball game that has ever been on television. Many of the children advance slowly at first.

Chad, who's on the other team and lives directly behind my back yard, dashes into my yard. A snowball strikes him immediately. His advance seemed hasty, but after more similar advances from his team, I realize their strategy.

Even if they have to go back to their base, they can remember how the forts, walls, and tunnels are formed. If they get lucky, they could even locate the coveted flag.

Chief runs throughout the enemy's territory, searching for the flag. He barks to tell his team where it is. Of course, they can't understand him. Too bad Chief isn't one of those new talking birds I've heard so much about.

The battle's momentum teeter-totters back and forth as the teams exchange barrages of snowballs. Each team has two players in jail. They watch the time anxiously, counting down the seconds until they can enter the combat again. I've been so enthralled by this game that, until now, I haven't noticed that Max is nowhere to be found. He would love to play in the snow.

Where is Max?

Not only that, but where are Tweedledee and Tweedledum? Both Max and the twins are gone. I'm the only cat around.

A quick look at all the trees doesn't reveal any cats watching the unfolding winter mayhem. Instead, I see barren trees, devoid of leaves, fruit, or cats. Except, of course, for the giant evergreen tree against the fence of the neighbors diagonally behind my back yard. The light orange trunk extends at least thirty feet into the sky until branches extend with green pine needles. The green catches my eye, but then I also notice something I've never seen before. There is an opening where one of the largest branches extends from the oddly lanky tree. Has that always been there? This is something I should inspect, but surely none of the other three cats are up there. So where are they?

This worries me. There are no animal tracks entering my domain, and so I don't think the Emperor could have already done something to Max or the twins. Am I just getting too paranoid in my old age?

I turn my attention back to the battle, and I see that Chad is sneaking next to Chief's pen. He's deep into my team's territory, and yet everybody on my team is either on the attack or pinned down elsewhere on the battlefield, dodging snowballs. I know it won't be long before Chad captures the flag and wins the game for the other team.

I dash down the tree, grab the flag in my mouth, and take it back up into the tree. It's against the rules for any of the players to move the flag, but cats are unfettered by typical rules. Besides, I'm the empress of the whole domain. I can move the flag if I want to.

From up in the tree, I watch Chad weave his way around my team's base. He frantically looks for the flag before my team spots him.

"Get Chad! Get Chad!" rings out from two of the kids coming back to our base. They've spotted Chad in our base, and they must think that Chad has the flag. Seconds later, my team surrounds Chad and pelts him with snowballs. He sulks back to his base without even seeing my team's flag. If only my team knew that I just saved the whole game for them.

I turn to head down the tree to put the flag near its original position, but as I do, I see Tweedledee leaving her people's house. She heads towards Grand Canyon Drive. Tweedledee moves quickly, and I need to catch her. My jaw drops open from surprise, and the flag falls out of the tree. I race down the tree, grab the flag, and put it back near where it had originally been. Then I race off towards the road to follow Tweedledee. At first, I see her tracks in the snow, but a deep rumbling noise sends me away from the road. A giant snowplow trundles past me down Rover Boulevard in the same direction I need to go. It plows snow, slush, and ice from the street onto the sidewalk. It covers the tracks. Tweedledee's trail has gone cold.

This is as good a time as any to go look at Grand Canyon Drive, I think to myself.

I MOVE QUICKLY down Rover Boulevard towards Grand Canyon Drive. I occasionally hear children playing in the snow in their yards, but in general, it is quiet. Nobody drives their cars on the snowy and icy roads, and so I can almost hear the snow falling to the ground around me.

The street I live on, Rover Boulevard, leads me eastward towards Grand Canyon Drive. Most of Rover Boulevard runs east and west, and Grand Canyon Drive runs north and south. Grand Canyon Drive is like a wall between the Emperor's domain and what is nominally mine. I only truly exercise control over the houses nearest me. Beyond that, all the way to Grand Canyon Drive there has not been a cat who has strongly exerted their own rule.

I approach Grand Canyon Drive. The snow is layered several inches thick on top of the street sign that labels this as Grand Canyon Drive.

Should I cross this Wall into the Emperor's territory? I wonder to myself.

If I'm stopped and questioned by one of the Emperor's servants, what would be my story? I can't say that I'm following a suspected spy.

Am I just becoming paranoid? I wonder.

I'm not sure if Tweedledee is even here; I did lose her trail. I walk along Grand Canyon Drive without crossing it so that I can look across and into the Emperor's territory. Although my side of the Wall is white with fresh snow, the Emperor's side has more black and gray. Cars have driven over Grand Canyon Drive despite the poor weather, and so there is dirt mixed in with the slush and ice. My domain remains a winter wonderland, whereas the Emperor's domain is drab. The houses are older. No children play in the snow.

Woof!

I instinctively dart up a nearby tree at the sound of a deep bark. It's a relatively small tree by the side of the road, but it should conceal me from the barking dog. What I then witness from up in the tree shocks me.

The dog is a German Shepherd. He chases a cat from the Emperor's territory onto Grand Canyon Drive. Halfway across, he overtakes the cat and captures it in his jaws. Seconds later, the German Shepherd is gone, having taken this cat back into the Emperor's territory.

I hear the snow falling softly around me. I blink my eyes, to check if what I saw truly happened. But I know that it did happen. I witnessed somebody trying to escape from the Emperor's domain, but was stopped at the Wall, Grand Canyon Drive.

Should I have intervened to save that cat? I wonder to myself.

But I can't fight off a German Shepherd. On the border of the Emperor's territory, my name and authority would not be recognized. I resolve to uncover the story of that cat.

What if that cat was the mole?

But not now.

I wait in the tree, listening to the snow and gazing as deeply as I can into the Emperor's territory. Once I'm sure that nobody is watching and I am about to take my first step down the tree, I see Tweedledee. She is crossing Grand Canyon Drive. She crosses the Wall into my territory without hindrance, in the exact same location where another cat was taken away by a German Shepherd just minutes ago. But Tweedledee crosses the Wall unmolested.

My first instinct is to run down and scold her, or to attack her for being a traitor, or to take her back to my domain for a trial. But something tells me to wait to find out the full story. She might be connected to the other cat somehow, and if I'm going to find out the truth, I might need Tweedledee a little bit longer.

Tweedledee continues down Rover Boulevard towards my territory.

How should I confront her when I get home?

Although I would love to vent my full anger at her, I decide I should just ask her some questions. We will see if her answers match up with what I know to be the truth.

———

"We showed them," the youngest girl child brags when I'm back home. "We totally won!"

The two younger children are peeling off layers of water-logged winter clothes.

"Yeah," the middle boy child says. "That was fun."

It must've been the most amazing fun in the world if the middle boy child shows this much enthusiasm. I snuggle under the buffet in the kitchen, and hot air blows out of the nearby register. This is my favorite spot during the winter.

The oldest girl child makes it out of bed and joins her siblings. I'm not sure if she's becoming more catlike in her teenage years, because she wants to sleep so much during the day.

"*Yawn.* What's with all the noise when I'm trying to sleep?" the oldest girl child asks.

"It was a miracle," the youngest girl child says. "Chad

should've found our flag, but for some amazing reason, he didn't see it, or he didn't take it, or something..."

"He walked right where the flag was," the middle boy child says.

"Did anybody call for me?" the oldest girl child asks.

"No," the big man person calls out from another room.

The younger children continue to excitedly retell how the game unfolded, but I don't listen because I see Max walking in from the garage. I permit him to join me under the buffet.

"Where have you been?" I ask as nonchalantly as I can.

"Hiding under the car in the garage," Max says.

"Really?" I say. "You would love playing in the snow. I thought you would've been the first one out there, leaping around in the snow like a crazy cat."

"I suppose you're right," Max says, "but maybe I'm just getting older. Once I heard the kids say, 'Snowball fight!' I wanted no part in that. I'm just not interested in fights anymore. I figure it's because of the battles we've had with Snarl and Patches. I'll go play in the snow now that there are no kids to hit me with snowballs."

Not a bad idea, I think to myself.

Although all of the children in my domain are kind, you never know when a teenager like Todd will wander by and unleash a volley of snowballs packed with ice and rocks.

"Good idea," I say. "I've got something to do, too." I go outside to go question Tweedledee.

I know Tweedledee's favorite spot to pee in her people's yard. I hide nearby to surprise her. It's not long before she comes out. I wait until she is just about to pee.

"You missed all the fun this morning," I say sharply. Tweedledee jumps as if she's pulling up her pants.

"You scared me—um, too bad," Tweedledee says. "I'm sure Max will play in the snow with me."

"Where were you?" I ask.

Tweedledee pauses to think. "I went to visit Gramma."

I need to get more information out of Tweedledee without being too pushy. She can't know I suspect her of being a traitor.

"I didn't know you had a grandmother to visit," I say. That statement will invite her to tell me more.

"Her health is failing," she says. "I try to visit once every few weeks."

"I thought I knew all the cats in my domain," I say. "I don't know of such a cat..."

I stare off into space as if I'm accessing the file cabinets of my memory. Tweedledee doesn't take the hint.

"What's her name?" I ask with all the empathy I can muster.

"I just call her Gramma. She lives far away. That's why you don't know about her."

"Where, exactly?"

"Up Rover Boulevard... Close to Grand Canyon Drive," she says, but then she abruptly shuts her mouth.

"In the Emperor's new territory?" I ask. "Perhaps she can help us."

"She's so old. And her health is failing. I don't think she could help. Besides, she lives close to Grand Canyon Drive, but not exactly in the Emperor's territory," Tweedledee clarifies.

Maybe Tweedledee had another errand besides visiting Gramma that took her into the Emperor's new territory. Or, perhaps, she's lying about where Gramma lives.

"I could come with you sometime," I suggest. "Next time I will go with you." I can't let Tweedledee know that I'm suspicious, so I halt the questioning.

"You missed a great capture the flag snowball fight game this morning," I say. "I saved the game from Chad." I then tell her the whole story, or at least as much as I know, about the capture the flag snowball fight. I don't mind repeating how I saved the game for my team.

3

It's now been a week since the big snow day, and I hear Chief let out a series of three short barks. It's our secret signal that he has something to tell me. Even though he can't be on the Cat Council, Chief is my most trusted adviser. He is a dog, but he's been alive for so long that he's managed to accumulate enough wisdom to be useful.

"What's up?" I ask Chief as I hop up onto the fence overlooking his pen. Chief doesn't say anything, but he nods to indicate I should come closer. I roll my eyes and hop into his pen towards his doghouse. He pushes out an empty can of cat food. A piece of paper is inside.

"What's this?" I ask.

"A message for you."

"From?"

"It was here when I woke up. I don't know."

"Have you read it?" I ask.

"It's addressed to you," Chief says. "Would I dare to read

Princess the Empress' private mail?"

He has a good point.

I unfold the letter and read it quickly. Its meaning is as clear as the clean glass windows Max tries to walk through. I need to take it somewhere else where Chief isn't watching me read it.

"What does it say?" Chief says.

"I could tell you," I say, "but then I would have to kill you."

Chief's eyes enlarge to the size of his food bowl.

"Just kidding," I say. The message, of course, is from the Emperor. This calls for an emergency Cat Council meeting. I tell Chief to pass the news to any of the other cats he sees. I go to tell Max.

The Cat Council meets like we always do. I sit at the front as the other three face me. None of them talk. The Emperor and all his spying has everybody scared.

The traitorous mole should be scared.

"Now that I've read the Emperor's note to you all," I say, "it is clear that we only have until New Year's Eve—less than three weeks—to comply with his demands. Of course, that will never be possible. There can only be one master, and he knows that. We will not submit like frightened mice."

"Why are you certain the Emperor is so bad?" Tweedledee asks. "The Emperor could be a very nice Emperor."

"Appeasement is not the way to victory. Appeasement would only give the Emperor more strength, power, and *bravado*. We must first resist."

"We need to attack right now, then," Tweedledum says. "We need to strike while his territory is still new, unstable, and unprepared to receive an attack."

Max's eyes dart between Tweedledee, Tweedledum, and me. He is clearly confused by this debate, and he would much rather be inside watching reruns of *M*A*S*H* on the people's television.

"Before we take action," I say, "we need to assess the Emperor's strength. He has a much larger area than I do. Remember, he did defeat the coyotes. Although, I would point out he was probably only able to do that because I first defeated Snarl. But there's more." I pause to make sure that everybody listens attentively. "The Emperor has weapons that we do not. We are, no doubt, cunning, fast, agile, and certainly able to defend our territory against common invaders. However, the Emperor has a weapon surpassing common."

The other three cats on the Cat Council exchange glances, wondering what this weapon could be.

"My own spy informs me that the Emperor has German Shepherds under his power." Of course, I don't tell them that I am the source of that information, and that I saw a German Shepherd with my own eyes. Whoever the mole is on my Cat Council, news of my imaginary agent will vex the Emperor like tree sap in his fur.

"We can't simply attack the Emperor and claim territory for ourselves," I say. "We would not be able to stand against German Shepherds." Tweedledum looks down to concede the point. "But as I said earlier, nor can we sit back and wait."

"Did you pee on the note yet?" Max asks.

"That is our most important card to play now," I say. "We need this mole to come through for us." I shift the paper note to the edge, squat over it, and soak it in urine. The four of us watch as words appear on the page as if by magic. It clearly reads: "Watch out for the Emperor's German Shepherds guarding the border."

This is perfect.

The mole has corroborated the information I already saw. This makes the mole trustworthy.

"We must not do anything rash," I say. "There is time until New Year's Eve to ponder and deliberate. Until then," I say, "be on guard. Do not trust anybody, and if anything new shows up, raise the alarm."

Once we all disperse from the meeting, Tweedledum comes up behind me and says, "We need to talk."

"I wasn't at the snowball fight because I was busy doing something important," Tweedledum says. "I was inspecting the house the new neighbors will be moving into."

"What did you discover?" I ask.

"More like, 'Whom?'" Tweedledum says. "During the snowball fight, I followed Max into their empty garage. In there, he acted really goofy. He ran around in circles and chased imaginary bugs. He was just plain loopy." I have a feeling I already know what Tweedledum is getting at.

"After a bit, Max fell asleep in their garage," Tweedledum says, "and I searched the garage." Tweedledum pauses.

I look at him as if to say, "And what did you find?"

"Max has a giant stash of catnip in that garage," Tweedledum says. "That much catnip is no good for any cat," Tweedledum says. "The question is: how in the world did he get all of that catnip? Why is he keeping it secret?"

"Thanks for telling me," I say to Tweedledum. "I will take care of it. You don't worry about a thing." But I'm worried about Max. Max is the traitorous mole, and he's being paid with catnip to betray me.

However, I still don't trust Tweedledee and Tweedledum. Why didn't Tweedledum tell me sooner? Perhaps he is trying to throw me off the scent. Tonight my people are hosting a pet holiday party, one of their most poorly conceived ideas. However, this will provide more opportunity for me to uncover the mole in my midst.

———

"THIS WILL BE SO EXCITING," the youngest girl child exclaims.

"It is going to be cool," the oldest girl child confirms.

The middle boy child grunts in agreement.

"When is everybody going to get here with their pets?" the oldest girl child asks her parents.

"They'll get here when they get here," the big man person says as he adds water to the Christmas tree in the living room.

My people have decided to host a pet holiday party at my house this year. I'm a bit chagrined they didn't bother to ask my permission. The youngest girl child came up with the idea of having a pet holiday party. All the guests will bring their pets with them to the party.

Does my house look like a zoo to anyone?

After dinner, the Christmas tree glows with brilliance, and Christmas music plays in the background.

Tweedledee and Tweedledum's family is the first to arrive. Chad and his parents carry them in. Tweedledee excitedly prances about once placed on the floor. She inspects the Christmas ornaments. Tweedledum is much less enthusiastic and stays near Chad.

"You just wait for the next snow day," Chad says to my children people. "You guys cheated. I'll get your flag next time."

"We didn't cheat," the youngest girl child says.

"It's not our fault you're blind," the middle boy child says. Their argument continues, but then Chief arrives with his people. Now that I think about it, I don't remember the last time I saw Chief's owners. All of their older children no longer live at their house. They are off at a place they mysteriously call, "college." I can't wait until some people in my family go to college.

The man walks slowly, like Chief, and maybe that's why Chief's not in good shape, either. He obviously doesn't take Chief for walks anymore. The woman, however, is light on her feet and talkative.

"We had to get here early so that he could get all the eggnog he wanted," she comments. I look over, and I see that he is already sipping a cup of eggnog. There is a reason one of the holiday rules I give to other cats is to never drink the eggnog.

I lay under the Christmas tree so that none of the other pets bother me. All of the children are playing and watching Christmas movies in another room, and all of the big people talk about subjects of the utmost importance.

Ding, dong. Ding, dong.

"I wonder who that could be," the big woman person says.

"Remember?" the big man person says. "We invited that new family moving in to come over."

That turns out to be just the case. Two adults enter the house, but to my relief, they don't have any animals with them.

"Did he tell you it's a pet holiday party, and that you were welcome to bring any of your pets along for the fun?" the big woman person asks. "He sometimes forgets to mention important details like that, you know."

"I told them," the big man person says in his own defense.

"He told us," the neighbor woman says. "But we're too busy packing up our old house, and we wanted as little disruption as possible."

"Sorry, but it's just us tonight," the neighbor man says.

Everybody introduces themselves to the new neighbors. They all shake hands, and the party resumes. Chief's owner man belches quietly and wipes his chin as he nurses yet another cup of eggnog.

The youngest girl child enters with the other children and announces: "Let's do the first game!"

Everybody else thinks that's a good idea, and they follow her instructions to sit in a circle with their pet.

"Okay," she continues. "Everybody needs to say their favorite thing about their pet."

I roll my eyes as I anticipate what people will say about Max.

"Mom," the oldest girl child continues, "you can start by sharing your favorite thing about Princess."

"Well," she stammers. "Let me think…"

She should be able to list many superlatives about me faster than a dog chasing a food truck. I'm offended she has to think for a few seconds. I get up, let out a grunt, and leave the living room. I go sit under an end table near my eating room.

Some people thought that was funny. I listen from the other room as the twins' owners talk about them. Tweedledum walks into the family room where I am.

I am going to put my brilliant plan into action. I will tell Tweedledum a false piece of information. If the Emperor acts on it, then I will know that Tweedledum is the mole.

"Come over here, Tweedledum," I say. "I've got something really important to tell you, and you can't tell the others about it."

Tweedledum comes over. "What?"

"Do you remember that last message we got from the

mole?" I ask.

"You mean about the German Shepherds?" Tweedledum asks.

"Yes, that's the one. That was only part of the message." Tweedledum squints as he looks like he's about to ask a question. I continue before he has a chance. "I didn't want everybody to know what the whole message from the mole was. The rest of the message said that I have to meet the mole at the old, abandoned gas station tonight at 10 PM."

I hear the people talking from the other room about Chief now. "Chief prevents vermin from moving into his doghouse. I guess that's one good thing about Chief."

I'm disgusted at how little the people my domain appreciate the animals that they call their pets.

Tweedledum starts talking to me, but I'm not paying attention to him. Instead, I'm listening to what the new family says about their pet.

"Our pet is so smart. She is the smartest pet ever. One time," the woman explains, "she got out of the locked room, but then broke into another locked room to steal food. Who has a pet that smart?"

Well, I think to myself, *I'm the smartest animal ever, so...*

Tweedledum is done talking, and I have no idea what he said because I was listening to what the new neighbors had to say about their pet, and so I simply say, "We can talk more later."

I can hear Chief snoring from the other room, and I peek back into the living room where the party is located. Max and Tweedledee play like kittens around the Christmas tree as the children egg them on. Chief's owner gulps down yet another cup of what I assume is eggnog. I'm not sure, but I think his stomach has gotten larger since he arrived. I wish this party would end. Tweedledum paces around.

Perhaps he is impatient and wants to tell the Emperor about my fake meeting with the mole at 10 PM. Then I would know that Tweedledum is the mole.

"Gift time!" the youngest girl child announces. The people gather back into the living room. They all grab a gift from under the tree, gifts that they brought with them, and place them in the middle of the room.

"This is a white elephant gift exchange," the oldest girl child explains. "Everybody brought a useless item from their home. When it's your turn, you pick one gift in the middle, or you steal a gift that somebody has already opened. Once a gift has been stolen twice, it cannot be stolen again."

The youngest girl child in my family goes first because she's the youngest. She's disappointed to unwrap a half empty jar of mayonnaise.

Not a bad gift, I think to myself.

The middle boy child is excited to open up a toy robot on his first chance.

"I hope nobody steals from me," the boy says as he looks around at everybody else who still has a turn-and a chance to steal from him.

Chad opens a box of chocolates. The oldest girl child groans once she pulls her gift out of the box: it is the ugliest Christmas sweater ever. It's red and green with gold sparkles, and it even has dangly-yarn things on the front. It rivals the emissary's ugly Christmas sweater. I don't pay attention to the rest of the game, but some of the better gifts include a set of walkie-talkies that the middle boy child steals after one of the adults steals his robot. The oldest girl child is trying to get a portable tape recorder that can play cassette tapes, but it can also record onto cassette tapes.

Just as a gift is about to be revealed, the house goes completely dark, and the music stops. The people gasp in surprise, and then the big man person concludes, "I guess the power went out. Maybe there is a big ice storm somewhere." The big man person stumbles around to find flashlights and candles. The children find them first.

Just as they light a candle, the lights come back on. Everybody blinks their eyes to adjust to the new light, and the party continues just as it had before. I don't see what the last gift is, because I notice that Tweedledum is gone.

I RACE through my eating room, into the garage, and then into my front yard. I hop up to the fence, and I look around. Should I go directly to the street, or should I go to my backyard into Tweedledum's yard? I go out to the street first, but I don't see anything.

I rush back through my backyard and into Tweedledum's yard. I make it out to his street, but I don't see anything suspicious. The snow has melted too much, and now it's frozen over. There are no fresh tracks visible in the snow. Tweedledum has escaped, and I don't know where he went.

I saunter back into the house as I ponder the possibilities. Perhaps Tweedledum said something to one of them.

All of the people are passionately involved in their white elephant gift exchange.

"I want the barrel of popcorn," the youngest girl child whines. "I love the cheese and caramel popcorn together."

"The buttered popcorn is the best," the oldest girl child counters.

"You can steal it back later," the big man person says. "Now pick your next gift." This gift exchange is apparently dramatic enough to keep everybody's attention.

I catch Max's eye, and I nod towards the other room. He gets up and makes his way towards me. I enter my eating room to question him. Once Max joins me in the eating room, I peek out to make sure that nobody followed us.

"Did Tweedledum say where he was going?" I ask.

"No. How should I know?"

I take note that Max answered a question with a question. This is a common tactic of evasion, something the mole would do.

"Did you see where he went?"

"Wait," Max says, "did Tweedledum go somewhere?"

"In case you didn't notice," I say, "he snuck away while the power was out."

"He did say that he did not want to be here," Max says.

"That's it?" I ask. "He just said he didn't want to be here?"

"Oh yeah," Max adds, "he also said he wanted to pee in your house to get you in trouble."

Doesn't Max realize my people would blame him, not me?

"If you had to guess, where do you think Tweedledum went?" I ask.

"*Hmmm,*" Max says as he looks at the ceiling. "I don't know. Maybe he just went home." That certainly is a possibility, I note to myself.

"What's with all these questions?" Max asks.

"His disappearance is suspicious."

"Do you suspect Tweedledum works for the Emperor?" Max

asks, wide-eyed. This is the most insightful thing Max has ever said. I don't think Max would be able to come up with it unless he was the mole himself, trying to evade detection.

"It's not safe for Tweedledum to be outside," I lie. "The Emperor could have agents out there..."

"Tweedledum does want your power, and so it wouldn't surprise me if he does work for the Emperor," Max says.

Max accused Tweedledum of being the mole.

This would be a brilliant tactic if Max were the mole himself.

I dismiss Max back to the holiday party, but I go outside to check on Tweedledum's house. Maybe he really was sick of the party. I circle his house on the fence that goes around the perimeter of his backyard, but I don't see Tweedledum.

I freeze and crouch down as I hear a metal tinkling sound nearby. I look to the front yard, and I see a German Shepherd trotting around the neighborhood. It doesn't see me, and it leaves just seconds later, heading towards Grand Canyon Drive. I'm not sure if it's the same German Shepherd that I saw before.

Did he meet with Tweedledum?

But Tweedledum is nowhere to be found. I head back to my house to question Tweedledee.

The white elephant gift exchange is still a roaring success. As I walk in, Chief's rotund owner gets up and says, "Time for another eggnog." As he tries to make his way through the group of people and gifts to get more eggnog, he trips on a gift and tumbles to the side. Max shows enough agility to avoid being crushed as he leaps and clings to the Christmas tree. An electrical cord snares Max, and lights on the Christmas tree blink on and off.

The Christmas tree teeters back and forth as Max looks

about frantically. The Christmas tree topples on its side, glass ornaments crunch as they break, and water splashes out of the base. Sparks dance about from the Christmas tree lights, a fire erupts from the tree, and the power goes out again.

Burp!

Chief's owner apparently just couldn't hold it in anymore.

"Too much eggnog!" Chief's woman owner scolds her husband as she covers her face in embarrassment.

All the children laugh at the chaos. My big man person runs in with a fire extinguisher, just as the smoke detector starts blaring its alarm. The extinguisher coats Chief's owner and the fallen Christmas tree in white foam.

As the people recover from the disaster, I nod to Tweedledee.

"Meet me in the other room," I whisper to Tweedledee. She gives a questioning look, but she follows me.

"Do you know where your brother is?" I ask.

"Who cares?" she answers. "He never plays with me anymore. He's always so busy."

"With what?"

"He says it's none of my business."

"Do you think he went to visit Gramma?" I ask.

"No," Tweedledee answers. "He doesn't care about her. Besides he wouldn't go... there," she says as she trails off right before she says her last word.

She must have remembered that she lied about the location of Gramma's house.

"Why do you care?" Tweedledee asks.

"Honestly," I say, "I'm concerned for his safety. The Emperor is encroaching on my territory." Now that I've spotted a German Shepherd this night, this is no stretch of the truth.

I dismiss Tweedledee back to the holiday party, and the rest of the evening passes without anything exciting happening. By the time everybody has gone back home, I've learned that the middle boy child won walkie-talkies in the white elephant gift exchange, and I can hear the youngest girl child playing with the miniature tape recorder that she won.

She never tires of making funny sounds, recording herself, and then playing it back for everybody else to hear. She also pretends to do a radio show about cats with Max.

I go outside to talk with Chief. I hop up onto the fence overlooking Chief's pen, but Chief asks me a question first.

"You know who your mole is?"

"Tweedledee goes to the Emperor's territory and lies about it," I say. "Max is receiving large payments of catnip and hides it. Tweedledum left the holiday party, probably to tell the Emperor how to catch his mole tonight at 10 PM." There's a few seconds of silence before I add, "So, no, I don't know who my mole is. I have reason to suspect all three."

Cats just can't be trusted.

"Who says you only have one mole?" Chief says. "Maybe everybody on your esteemed Cat Council is working against you."

I'm stunned by this possibility.

"Have you spotted any other cats or dogs?" I ask with the German Shepherd still in my mind.

Chief lifts his nose into the air and gives a few sniffs, but he shakes his head to indicate that he senses nothing.

Perhaps the Cat Council tomorrow and the new neighbors moving in will reveal something. I am also expecting another message from the mole in an empty can of cat food.

4

"The main thing to remember," I tell Max, Tweedledee, and Tweedledum at the Cat Council the next day, "is that we must not talk to that bird." I don't trust that bird. An animal that can talk with other animals and people is not to be trusted. That is a power not meant to be yielded by animals.

"One of our main goals during moving day is to gauge their acceptance of animals, and especially cats like us," I say. "We want to set their expectations so that they will not think anything is out of place if we"-I really mean me-"are in their yard whenever we want to be."

The other three cats on the Cat Council nod their heads.

"Look out for anything sinister from the Emperor," I remind them. "It can't be a coincidence that the family moving out of the Emperor's newly acquired territory just so happens to be moving into my territory." Again, they all nod their heads with understanding.

I don't tell them, but I will also be looking for more empty cans of cat food. This is how the mole told me he would communicate with me.

Max and I go on the first patrol while the new neighbors start to move into their house. They've backed up a vehicle like a delivery truck onto the driveway, and they're emptying it into the house.

The neighbors unceremoniously dump Max's catnip into garbage bags, assuming it's junk from old occupants. Not knowing what it is, the new neighbor lady takes bag after bag full of catnip out of the garage and puts it in a garbage barrel.

I have not decided how to confront Max about his catnip secret. I see Max try to hold back tears, but I pretend not to notice. Max and I make our way around the house, and the first thing we notice is that these new people, as far as we can tell, don't appear to have any young children. Also, these people are ignoring us so far.

"I think there might be some more catnip in the back corner of the garage," I tell Max. With uncharacteristic boldness, Max saunters in towards the back of the garage.

"Shoo! Shoo!" the new lady neighbor says, swinging the broom at Max. He runs out and says to me, "Hey! There is no catnip in there."

"Sorry," I say. "Honest mistake." We get as close as we can to the truck and unloaded belongings, but I don't yet see any empty cans of cat food that would have a message from the mole.

I lead Max back to Chief's pen where we meet up with Tweedledee and Tweedledum.

"Your turn, guys," I say. "Max and I will watch from back here."

Just as Tweedledee and Tweedledum make their way towards the house, another car shows up. This time, what I can only describe as semi-adults get out of the car. This new family apparently has three boys, all older than the oldest girl child of my people. One is quite a bit older, and I suspect he may have the same thing my big man person has: a job. The other two boys are slightly younger, but they look exactly the same. They must be twins.

The three boys ceremoniously carry a large covered object into the house. I can't discern what it is, but the three boys are careful not to jostle whatever is under the cover. I hope Tweedledee and Tweedledum find a way to discover what was in that concealed item. While they do, there's something else I need to inspect.

"Watch the twins as best you can from here," I tell Max. "I need to stretch my legs for a bit and tend to a few things. I'll meet you back here soon."

When Max has his eyes trained on the house Tweedledee and Tweedledum are infiltrating, I shimmy thirty feet up the nearby evergreen. This tree is huge, but since it has so few needles for such a large tree, I often don't notice it's here. My curiosity has gotten the best of me; I want to know about that opening high up in the tree, and I can't stand to watch the twins' bumblings accompanied by Max's commentary.

After my initial burst up the tree, my legs burn from the physical exertion. I look down.

I definitely wouldn't want to fall from here.

But then I look up. I still have a ways to go.

My claws are about to fall out of my paws when I finally pull myself up on to the first large branch of the evergreen. I don't care about the opening right now. I care about catching my breath and giving my muscles a rest. Between deep breaths that pull in the chilly Christmas-time air, I dare to look down again. I get slightly dizzy when I see Max, who is now the size of a bug.

I force myself to look away from the ground far below, and I look into the opening in the evergreen tree. I was right: there is indeed an opening. I have no idea how long it has been there. Perhaps it has been there my whole life. Right now, I don't care, because it's not empty.

Two giant eyes stare out at me from inside the tree, and a hissing sound is released. My instincts force my fur on end and my exhausted claws to extend. At this altitude on this tiny branch, I have no desire to fight anybody. I just want to get down this tree.

A flurry of squeaks and squawks nearly startles me off the branch.

"Who?" comes the challenge. "Who are you?" A round feathered face leans out of the opening, and the two giant eyes shrink slightly in suspicion.

An owl.

"I am Princess, Empress of Rover Boulevard, Slayer of the Wicked Coyote, Snarl. This tree is in my domain. Who are you?"

"Moonbeam, the owl. I just moved here after much searching for a new home, but finding none."

We stare at each other. I'm deathly afraid he'll force me to fall out of the tree, stranded up so high on this solitary branch. He must be afraid I'll try to eat him.

"Welcome to my domain," I say. "I'm going to climb down now." I slowly walk along the branch towards the trunk. Moonbeam settles back into his concealed nest. I go down the large trunk headfirst. The ground races towards me, and I slow my descent.

"What did I miss?" I ask Max when I'm back by his side. He's too engrossed to hear me. The twins trot in our direction. I know an owl has arrived in my domain, but can the twins tell me what was in the covered object?

The twins don't disappoint me.

"It's a talking bird, all right," Tweedledum says. "It was covered at first, but we were close enough to look through the window, and we saw them unveil it. We couldn't hear anything for sure, but we could see the people's mouths moving as they looked at the bird, and we could see the bird's beak move some as it looked back."

"The bird does have a cage, but it seems like it doesn't have to stay in it," Tweedledee says. "We saw it go all about the house, able to look out the front windows, the back windows, and the side windows. It can see everything easily."

"Did you try to talk to it?" I ask.

"No," Tweedledee and Tweedledum answer in unison.

"But I do think the bird saw us just as we were leaving," Tweedledum says.

"Good job, guys," I say. "That's important information about this family."

"I will go on one last patrol alone," I tell the others. "Stay here."

I go to the neighbor's house, and my eyes scan about, looking for the message from the mole. I realize that I've never been inside the truck itself. Except for a few odds and ends, the truck's bay is empty. It's the only place I have not looked for a message from the mole, and so I hop up into the cargo bay of the truck. I go all the way into the dark back, desperate to find his message.

A loud metallic grating sound turns my head, and then —*SLAM*! Somebody slammed the door of the truck shut. I'm trapped in the truck. But then I see it. There's an empty can of cat food in the opposite corner. Inside, I find a folded piece of paper. As I unfold the note, the truck engine rumbles to life. I feel the truck back up and then drive forward. Before I have a chance to read what's in the note, I realize that this truck is probably taking me to the people's old house beyond Grand Canyon Drive to reload. Whether I like it or not, this truck is taking me to the Emperor's new territory and his German Shepherds.

———

THE TRUCK TRUNDLES down Rover Boulevard. I don't know exactly when, but at some point we must cross the Wall, Grand Canyon Drive, into the Emperor's new domain.

After a few turns, I feel the truck hit a little bump and then slow down. I grab the note left by the mole in the old cat food can, and I crouch behind a bucket near the door.

There's a click, and then the door of the cargo bay slides up, allowing sunlight to stream in. The man heads into his house to get more stuff to put in.

I hop out to go hide under a nearby bush. I plan to sneak back into the truck to ride home after the man is nearly finished loading it.

But there's a slight breeze, and it brings a foul odor: German Shepherds. My keen ears then pick up the low and gruff voices of several German Shepherds having a discussion nearby.

Thankfully, I'm downwind of them, so I know they can't smell me. I peer through the cracks of the fence and see several German Shepherds grouped together.

I silently leap on top of the fence to look down on four German Shepherds. One of them is clearly in charge.

"Congratulations on catching Fluffy," the leader says. "Nobody will hear from Fluffy again. *Ha, ha!*"

"Thank you, Otto," says one of the other German Shepherds.

"You three remember," Otto the leader continues, "that the Emperor wants continued safe passage for that cute white kitten named Tweedledee."

"But me and Gunther would love to catch that nice little kitty," growls one of the others.

"Hey, Hans," another says, "not if Herman is able to catch her first." The three other German Shepherds break out in laughter.

"Silence!" Otto orders. Once there's stillness, he continues. "I don't understand the orders, either. I just give them. Nobody touches Tweedledee, or you will face the wrath of the Emperor." Everybody else is quiet and nods their heads in understanding.

"In addition to that," Otto continues, "we must be vigilant. There is a spy in the Emperor's territory. There is a spy undermining the authority of our master, the Emperor. We must be wary."

"Yes, master," the other three dogs bark in unison.

So there is a spy working against the Emperor, but he knows about it!

This both excites and worries me. However, it also means the Emperor hasn't caught his mole.

"I can't wait until we catch that spy," one of the German Shepherds growls. "Me and Hans will rip him to shreds."

"All of us will rip him to shreds," Otto corrects the other German Shepherd.

"Next item on the agenda..." Otto continues, but I look back, and I see that the truck is mostly full. I need to get back in the truck, or I will risk being stranded in the Emperor's territory.

I leap down from the fence and rush over to the truck. I hop up into the cargo bay, and I work my way amongst all of the boxes away from the entrance of the bay to make sure that I'm out of sight. This is ending up to be a good detour into the Emperor's territory.

My breathing has slowed down now that I'm safely inside the truck. The big man person has the truck almost completely full. I allow myself to exhale a deep breath knowing that I should be back in my own territory soon. The man heads back into his house, but then I see something leap up onto the back edge of the truck. I can't see clearly what it is, and so I angle my head. It's the Emperor's messenger, or emissary, as he likes to be called.

"Princess," the emissary calls out. "I know you're in here."

I leap out of my hiding spot, and I bolt towards the exit of the truck opposite the side that the emissary is in. I can't be trapped in here. The emissary shows uncharacteristic strength and agility, and he leaps over and blocks me into the wall of the truck.

I back up. I'm trapped. I puff up all of my fur, and I arch my back, but I'm careful not to hiss. Doing so would alert the German Shepherds. The emissary does the same. His back is arched, his claws are out, and his fur puffs up around his sweater. If the emissary raises the alarm, there is definitely no hope I could out run the German Shepherds. I only have one chance now that the emissary has trapped me.

"I have much to offer you," I say as smoothly as I can. "I can offer you many more sweaters. I can offer you all the catnip you could ever want," I say as I ponder Max's piles of catnip that are now in a garbage bin back in my territory. I consider offering him power in my domain, but I decide against it. "The Emperor doesn't treat you as well as he should, does he? Work with me instead, and you can have all of these riches." I know my offer is weak, but I don't have any other choice in this situation.

The emissary pauses. He shrinks back to normal size, and he tilts his head as he looks at me. He then says, "What else can you give me?" And then he lets out a chuckle.

This puzzles me. I can't believe he accepted.

What else can I offer him? The best sunning spot in my house?

"I'm the mole," the Emperor's emissary says. "I'm the one who can help and wants out."

5

"Follow me," the emissary and supposed mole says. He hops off the back of the truck and goes to the other side of the house, away from the German Shepherds.

That crazy cat! I think to myself.

Half of me wants to stay in the truck, but I know I can't. I walk to the edge of the truck, listen to make sure the German Shepherds are still involved in their own discussion, and then I follow behind the emissary to the other side of the house. Once we're under a small bush, I ask, "Why didn't you tell me you're the mole at the Cat Council?"

"You have a traitor in your midst," the emissary says. "I couldn't risk exposing myself in front of the traitor."

"Why are you doing this?" I ask. "Why are you risking your life for me?"

"For *you*? Don't think for a second I'm doing it for you. Now listen here," he says as he leans in. "The man person is in the bathroom doing his business, but even that won't give me enough time to explain all of it."

"Explain what you can," I say.

"Basically, the Emperor has been controlling me through my brother, Fluffy. My brother resisted the Emperor's power in subtle ways. He saw that the Emperor is not a kind ruler. He abuses power, he bends the rules for his benefit, and things that made him look bad are swept under the rug. When the Emperor expanded his territory to Grand Canyon Drive, my brother tried to escape. He had proof that the Emperor murdered the cat who used to be in charge of Grand Canyon Drive."

I knew Mozart *disappeared because of the Emperor.*

"But," the emissary continues, "one of those German Shepherds caught him just as he was crossing Grand Canyon Drive."

That's what I saw when I tried to follow Tweedledee.

"Come with me in the truck back to my territory," I say. "You can be safe in my territory, and tell me everything I need to know to defeat the Emperor."

"I can't leave," the emissary says, "until I have done all that I can to save my brother. The German Shepherd didn't kill my brother. He was put into the Emperor's prison. All who defy the Emperor, and even many who have not, end up in that prison. I can't abandon my brother. I need to continue to work here against the Emperor for my brother. Really, for everybody in that prison."

"Who is the Emperor?" I ask. "I thought I knew all of the cats, even the ones who are from farther away."

"The Emperor may not be a cat," the emissary says. "Nobody knows. What we do know is that the Emperor is ancient, and nobody is allowed into his presence."

"How can he run his empire?" I ask. "How can he control everybody so effectively?"

"He communicates to his dog subjects," the emissary answers, "and they obey him without question. It's like mind control, somehow. The dogs under his control are powerful. Who could hope to stand up against German Shepherds?"

"Of course German Shepherds are strong, but how can he control German Shepherds?" I ask. "Why don't the German Shepherds just work for themselves instead of submitting to the Emperor?"

The emissary's answer makes everything clear for me, and the shock of it makes me lose my breath for a second.

"The Emperor has the power of human speech, and he commands the dogs like a human master."

I know immediately that the Emperor is the new neighbor's pet bird, who has the ability to speak not only with other animals but also by using human speech. What's worse, the Emperor has just moved in to the house diagonally behind my own house.

"The Emperor is already in my territory," I say.

"Help me rescue my brother from prison," the emissary says.

"You know that's impossible," I say. "I can't get across the Wall and into the Emperor's territory, let alone rescue your brother, or anybody else, from the Emperor's prison. That's crazy! I need to defeat the Emperor back in my own neighborhood."

"Promise to help me get my brother out of prison," the emissary says. Once again, I see his cunning peek out from behind his goofy cat sweater. "If you don't promise to help me get my brother out of prison, I'm going to call those German Shepherds right now, and you will find yourself in the Emperor's prison. If I'm able to capture you for the Emperor, then that will only make me more trustworthy to the Emperor."

I stare down the emissary, but he takes in a deep breath to shout for the German Shepherds.

"I will help rescue your brother," I say. The emissary gives me an intense look, and if it weren't for the seriousness of our situation, I would have to laugh looking at his goofy collar along with his Christmas cat sweater.

The emissary tells me when and where to expect empty cans of cat food with messages, and he also gives me one crucial clue about my traitor.

"The Emperor prefers to pay his agents who are cats with catnip," he says. "There's one lady in his domain who supplies all his catnip that he uses to pay his agents."

"Thank you," I say. "That is helpful." My heart sinks because I know Max has been receiving payments of catnip.

"To prove that I'm the mole, read the note I left for you in the truck," the emissary says. "It will tell you how and where to meet Jacques."

Before I have a chance to confirm what the emissary says, he disappears.

The man slams the house door shut and goes to the truck. I hurry over, and I watch the man pull the back of the cargo bay shut. He proceeds to get into the driver's seat and start the truck.

That truck is my only ride out of here!

I dash towards the truck, and I hope I'm fast enough to hop onto the back.

I will have to be fast enough to ride it back to my territory, because the emissary calls out, "Otto, Hans, Herman, Gunther! Intruder! Otto!"

I leap onto the back bumper of the truck as it pulls out of the driveway, and four German Shepherds barge out of the nearby yard. They chase, but the man accelerates the truck towards Grand Canyon Drive. The German Shepherds fade into the distance. I breathe a sigh of relief as we cross the Wall, and I arrive in my own territory. I'm a bit chagrined that the emissary called the German Shepherds, but I realize it was necessary for him to maintain his cover as a faithful and loyal subject to the Emperor.

Minutes later, the moving truck pulls into the driveway of my neighbor's house. Tweedledee and Tweedledum sit on the fence and watch. I hop off the bumper and hide nearby to retrieve the emissary's note inside the moving truck. I then hide the note under a lilac bush and go to my favorite sunbeam to relax and think. I will have to read the note later when the twins can't watch me.

Now that the Emperor is my neighbor, it won't be long before he makes a move.

THIS IS my chance to end all of this right now. The Emperor is in the new neighbor's house, and if that bird is the Emperor, I might as well sneak in there as soon as I can and get rid of him. I'm giddy about this possibility. The Emperor has made a great miscalculation by moving into my territory far too early, and without his defenses.

Me versus a bird? Easy.

Once night falls, as I have done many times in the past, I enter into the neighbor's garage through the hole that's only loosely covered by rocks. Then, all I have to do is wait until somebody opens the door so I can sneak into the house. The garage is full of boxes and odds and ends, and so it's easy to hide while I wait. I only need that door open for a split second.

I don't have to wait long before the garage door opens, and light streams in from the rest of the house. Christmas decorations illuminate the house, and Christmas music pours into the garage. The man flips on the light switch, takes a few steps in, grabs a beverage from a case, and goes back into the house. Just as the man shuts the garage door, I slide a piece of cardboard from one of their used moving boxes into the doorway. It prevents the door from shutting completely.

I wait a few seconds, and then I open the door a crack and peek in. The house, like the garage, is full of boxes and random household items. The man and the woman are talking. I sneak into the house, and I use the moving boxes as cover to hunt for the Emperor.

"Let's get this all unpacked and be done with it," the man says, and then he takes a swig from his beverage.

"Christmas only comes one time a year," the woman says, "and so we are going to decorate for Christmas, even if everything is not unpacked yet."

"Fine," the man says, and I can practically hear his eyes roll in his head. The Christmas music playing right now is about some silly snowman that comes to life, but I don't let that distract me from searching the house for that evil bird.

I search two bedrooms, but both of them only have a few boxes in them with the names of their sons written on them. There's no bird. I sneak my way to the far end of the house, and as I approach what I guess to be a living room, I have a sense that this must be the Emperor's room. It's darker, and the Christmas music is softer at this end of the house. I wonder if the Emperor is resting right now. My eyes adjust to the light, and I'm confident that the dim light will give me an advantage. I stealthily sneak into the room to locate the bird. The fur on my neck stands up.

The Emperor is somewhere in this room.

"Halt!" A human man's voice rings out. "Who goes there?"

I dive for cover behind a partially unpacked box.

"Oh," the parrot says in animal talk. "It's only you, Princess, the so-called empress of these lands. But not anymore. As you can see, I've moved in now. *Ha, ha, ha.*"

"As you can see," I counter, "there are no German Shepherds in here to do your bidding. And this empress is at the top of the food chain."

I leap into the center of the room and attack the first thing that moves. A bird has no chance against me in this small room. After a few leaps about the room—aided by some of the taller boxes—towards the fluttering wings, I nearly have him. I feel a rush come into my heart as I sense my prey nearing its doom.

"Help! Help!" a woman's voice calls out in the room. "He's hurting me! He's hurting me!"

I swipe at this bird, but I realize too late that this parrot is about as large as I am, and its talons are sharp and strong. The Emperor is a large parrot, and he draws blood, but most of my slashes have only found air.

"Police!" a man's human voice calls out. "Police! Stranger danger," a child's voice calls out this time.

The lights come on in the room, momentarily blinding me before my eyes adjust. The man trips over me and spills his beverage as I turn to dash out of the room. I race across the house to the garage, pass the woman nursing a beverage, and I praise myself for having left the cardboard sticking in the garage door so that I can escape. I sprint out of the garage and go back to my own yard.

I imagine the man protectively coddling his evil parrot inside his home, so concerned for its safety and well-being. Little does he know what a reign of terror his parrot has over the animal kingdom.

Snow is falling again. I'm thankful for the cold snowflakes to rest against my hot, burning fur. The cold soothes the scratches I received from the talons of that parrot.

I missed an opportunity to end this conflict once and for all.

"What are you doing, Max?" I call out to Max, who is under the lilac bush where I left the note.

"I found a note," Max explains with a stutter in his voice, "and I figured it was from that mole, so I peed on it..."

I look at the unnecessarily urine soaked note, and it tells me how to meet Jacques, just as the emissary said.

"I had to pee anyways," Max says. "And what happened to you?" Max must notice my ragged fur and heaving chest.

"Let's just say that the Emperor is more than a tweety bird."

My direct assault on the Emperor was not for nothing. I've confirmed that the Emperor does have the power of human speech. He could control dogs with his own voice. I heard the Emperor perfectly imitate many human voices. There's no doubt that the Emperor has learned the human voices of all of the German Shepherds' masters.

THE MOUSE SCURRIES away from me for its life, but I'm just playing with it. Chasing mice always makes me feel better, even if just for a minute. I probably won't end the mouse's miserable existence by playing with it and then eating it. I sometimes just need some distraction and amusement when I'm busy running my empire. But that twitching tail is so tempting...

As I'm about to make my last pounce, the mouse disappears in a blur. I take cover and look all around me, trying to discover what could have made the mouse vanish. My eyes finally catch Moonbeam perched on a fence post. He gulps down the mouse. I consider myself the best hunter in my domain, but I can't help but be in awe of this owl. In complete silence, he dove from the sky and snatched a mouse away from me.

"Impressive," I say.

Moonbeam does not say anything in response, but his two large eyes slightly rotate with the rest of his head.

"Completely silent and undetected. You are like a ninja of the sky."

"Ninja of the sky?" Moonbeam asks. "I like it."

"You are welcome in my domain," I say. "But why have you come? I only ask because I've had some unsavory guests in the past."

"My kin and I are protectors of the night. Unseen, and only felt when necessary. Right now, we face an invisible enemy that is decimating our numbers."

"Who could reach you in the sky, or so high up in the trees? Who could detect you, the silent ninjas of the night sky?"

"We don't know," Moonbeam says as he looks down at his feet. "We suspect something from the humans. The few of us who remain have spread out to find refuge. Somebody, or something, hunts us relentlessly, but so far it is a faceless enemy. We can't find homes, or we get mysteriously sick."

"You seek a new home for your family?" I ask.

"Not my family. My species. I am not fully grown yet. My

parents are dead. I only have an uncle, an older brother, and then a few more distant relatives."

With Moonbeam, I sense cunning—like a snake—but there's also a nobility and an independence that is like a cat. I feel a kindred spirit with this owl.

"Summon your kin," I say. "You and all of your kin are welcome in my domain. But, you must be aware that my domain has its own threats at the present moment that I cannot control."

Moonbeam holds my gaze for a second, and just as I wonder if he's going to reply, he says, "I've noticed."

Moonbeam launches silently into the night and disappears.

6

"I have gathered you all for an emergency Cat Council meeting," I say to the other three cats. "I have made some shocking discoveries. I'm still angry about my humiliating defeat inside the Emperor's new home. I am also sick and tired of thinking that the other cats in my domain are working against me."

I'm going to accuse all of them and see if I can uncover the mole. I'm not sure this is the smartest way to go, but my anger smolders against the mole.

"First. You, Max," I say as I bore my eyes into Max's. He averts his eyes from my piercing gaze. "You were paid in catnip to give secrets to the Emperor."

"What? But..."

I don't let him speak.

"You saved my life before, and so I assumed you were loyal to me. I don't know where you went astray. Perhaps you became jealous. Or the catnip was too enticing. How far you have fallen!"

"No," Max pleads, "it's not like that at all."

"How else could you have earned all of that catnip secretly?" I say.

"I don't know," Max stammers. "I just thought, I... I don't know. I guess I was blinded by my love for catnip."

"Nobody would give all that catnip for nothing," I say.

"Please, Princess..." Max grovels.

"If I may," Tweedledee says quietly as she tentatively holds up her paw, "I do have something to say."

This raises my ire. I turn my gaze to her to accuse her.

"You lied to me as well," I say. "Max kept his giant payment of catnip hidden, but you lied to my face."

"What are you talking about?" Tweedledee asks.

"I watched you cross Grand Canyon Drive the other day."

Tweedledee's white face turns red.

"How did you see me?" Tweedledee asks.

"None of your business," I say. "You told me you were coming home from visiting Gramma, who lives on this side of Grand Canyon Drive. But you crossed Grand Canyon Drive. That's something the Emperor's spy would do."

"That detail about where Gramma lives, it doesn't matter. I didn't want you to be suspicious."

"There's more," I say. "I've been into the Emperor's new territory. And I overheard his border guards, those fierce German Shepherds."

All three of the other cats shake with fear, probably wondering how I obtained information from German Shepherds.

"Those German Shepherds have explicit orders from the

Emperor to give you, Tweedledee, free passage in and out of his domain."

Both Max and Tweedledum stare at Tweedledee with gaping mouths.

"And that is nothing to scoff at," I add. "Because earlier I witnessed an innocent cat trying to escape out of the Emperor's new territory. He bolted across Grand Canyon Drive, but one of those German Shepherds chased after him, snatched him up, and pulled him unwillingly back into the Emperor's domain. If he's lucky, he's in one of the Emperor's prisons. If he's not lucky, then..."

All three of the other cats huddle together in horror from my accusations. This is going wonderfully well from my perspective.

"So, why does the Emperor give you safe passage?" I ask Tweedledee. Even Max knows this is a rhetorical question and remains quiet. "It's because you work for the Emperor."

The accusation sits in the cold air amongst the four of us, and Tweedledee has nothing to say in her defense. She trembles, on the verge of crying. Tweedledum eventually speaks up timidly.

"I would like to make an announcement," Tweedledum says. But now it's time for me to accuse Tweedledum.

"You remember the night of the holiday party, don't you?" I ask Tweedledum. Tweedledum furls his brow at the question. "I tricked you and told you that we were going to meet the mole that very night at 10 PM at the abandoned old gas station. You were the only one I told."

"So what?" Tweedledum says. "Why would you tell a lie like that?"

"You work for the Emperor, too," I say. "You alone had that

juicy morsel of information. You had to get back to the Emperor, or Otto, his head German Shepherd, in time for him to catch the mole by 10 PM that night. Don't think I didn't notice you snuck out when the electricity went off. You no doubt left to go tell the Emperor."

"That's not why I left," Tweedledum says.

"It's just a coincidence you had to leave right when I gave you a crucial and timely piece of information?"

"Let me explain..."

"Just try," I challenge Tweedledum. At this point, I'm ready to throw all three of these buffoons out of Cat Council permanently as traitors, pending further punishment. Nobody in my kingdom has ever committed such heinous crimes!

"I left to see the girl I'm going to marry," Tweedledum says. "It's been a secret, but we're in love, and that's why I've snuck away at various times. I don't want anything to do with the power struggles that go on around here. I'm leaving you all for love. If it matters to you all, her name is Tinkerbell. Don't worry, I will be moving far to the west with Tinkerbell."

Tweedledum looks each of us in the eye in turn, but his eyes linger the longest on Tweedledee, who is crying now.

"I love you, sis," Tweedledum says, "but I need to leave."

Tweedledum trots away from the Cat Council.

The rest of us sit stunned. Seconds later, Tweedledee must realize what's happening, and she runs after her brother. But she returns only minutes later, alone. Tweedledee covers her eyes with her paws, but she can't contain the tears over her lost brother. Max is stunned and sits still with his mouth open. I don't know what to do. Is Tweedledum lying, and I should go chase him down and drag him back as a traitor? Or, did Tweedledum really leave so that he could see his girlfriend?

"I'm so sorry, I'm so sorry," Tweedledee says through her sobs. "I'm the one who has been bringing the catnip for Max."

"What?" I ask Tweedledee.

"Gramma has me bring catnip, and she told me to put it in that garage. She wouldn't explain why. She just makes me do it for her without asking any questions. I'm the one who's been bringing all that catnip and putting it in the garage. I guess Max must have found it."

Tweedledee continues crying, and Max confirms: "Yeah, I just found it."

Tweedledum could be innocent, and Max and Tweedledee could merely be unwitting accomplices of the Emperor. The Emperor must have planned all of this to tear my domain apart from the inside.

———————————

THE GARBAGE TRUCK rumbles away from my people's house the next morning.

Farewell, message, I think to myself. *May you find your intended recipient.*

Just as the emissary and I agreed, I put a note in a marked cat food can, and I left it with my people's trash for the trash man to haul away. If Jacques does his job, the note will make its way to the emissary with directions for my next step in the plan. I go to the twins' yard, reminding myself that it's now only Tweedledee's yard. Chad and his parents probably have not yet noticed that Tweedledum is missing.

"Why?" Tweedledee asks with puffy red eyes and a hoarse throat.

"You need to visit Gramma tonight," I say. "I will go with you."

"We can't do that," Tweedledee says. "It's too dangerous. I had no idea German Shepherds were watching me, and that I was only spared because of the Emperor's plan."

"The Emperor still wants his catnip delivered," I say. "The Emperor has no reason to think the catnip deliveries should stop. Besides, it is essential that I talk to Gramma." I'm almost certain that the Emperor's plan with the catnip was to confuse me. He set things up so that I thought both Tweedledee and Max were working against me.

"Okay..." Tweedledee says with a hint of reluctance. "But that will draw some suspicion."

"True, but—"

"The German Shepherds will surely grab you at the border," Tweedledee interrupts. "Remember, the Emperor granted safe passage for me, not for everybody with me."

"Don't worry," I assure her. "I have a plan. We will not go alone. I need to go talk to somebody else. We'll meet again tonight."

I leave Tweedledee so I can nap before my next meeting. My house is quiet until late in the afternoon. Tomorrow is the beginning of Christmas break for my people, and the children are thrilled to have several weeks off from school.

The oldest girl child plans to have a sleepover with friends. However, I know she is planning more than just a sleepover.

When her parents haven't been listening, I've heard her talking on the phone with her friends. They say they're just going to stay up late and watch Christmas movies, but I know there are going to sneak out of the house late at night. They're going to a late night party at a house across Grand Canyon Drive. They are my ticket into the Emperor's new territory.

After my meeting with my friend who will help us, I go to see Tweedledee again. I hope I don't stink like my friend I just talked with.

"We can't go tonight," she says. "It's too dangerous."

"Some of my people will be going across Grand Canyon Drive. When we go with my people, the German Shepherds will leave us alone. They wouldn't dare attack people."

Tweedledee can't argue with that

"I'm not just worried about us," Tweedledee says. "I'm worried about Gramma. Even if they don't harm us, Gramma is still in Emperor's territory, and I'm afraid of what he will do to her."

"I know exactly how we are going to lose those German Shepherds," I say. "They won't even know that we went to visit your Gramma. She'll be safe."

"Okay..." Tweedledee concedes.

"Trust me on this, Tweedledee," I say. "This is our only chance. Sneak out of your house after dark, and meet me. I will be with the oldest girl child and some of her friends."

The oldest girl child's sleepover starts off that evening just as she said it would. Three of her friends come over, and they order pizza. The arrival of the pizza delivery boy gets me thinking. A pizza delivery car would be an easy way to cross Grand Canyon Drive. I grow impatient as the girls watch movies. They have to wait until the big man person and the big woman person are in a deep sleep. It's obvious when they fall asleep because they both snore. I'm not sure how either of them sleeps with the other snoring so loudly.

After a movie ends, the parents' snoring resonates

throughout the whole house. The middle boy child is going to go with them as well. They have to go through his room to sneak out the window to go outside. I make my way through my eating room, out the garage, and then out to the front yard. I carry a small package to deliver to Gramma. Tweedledee joins me, and we watch the four girls and the boy quietly walk down the road. They carry a duffel bag with them, an odd choice for a party. Once they are several houses away, they start laughing and celebrating. I run to catch up with them, and Tweedledee follows.

"Princess," the oldest girl child says when she sees me. "What are you doing here? Go back home." I give her a look and continue walking.

"We can't go back just for a cat," the middle boy child says.

"Yeah," one of the girls says. "These cats will find their way home later." Tweedledee and I stay close, especially when we approach Grand Canyon Drive.

"We will almost certainly see German Shepherds," I say. "Just walk casually."

"What do you mean, 'Walk casually?'"

"I don't know. Just walk... *casually.*"

When we cross Grand Canyon Drive into the Emperor's territory, it somehow feels as if we are in a new world. I spot one set of golden eyes from a German Shepherd glaring at us. I was right. He does not dare move or attack a group of people. He licks his chops, probably in hopes that we separate from the people.

We will separate, but he won't be licking his chops for long.

AFTER SEVERAL MINUTES, we arrive at the party. It is not the party I expected. The house we stand in front of is silent and dark. The four girls and the middle boy child open their duffel bag and snicker. They pull rolls of toilet paper out of the duffel bag.

With chuckles and grins, they throw the toilet paper all over the yard. They heave the rolls up into the trees, leaving streams of toilet paper hanging from nearly every branch. Tweedledee, of course, chases after the toilet paper. The people can hardly contain their joy. It's not long before toilet paper droops from every barren branch, covers the bushes, and crisscrosses the lawn. They even dare to throw some rolls of toilet paper into the backyard.

They are on their last roll of toilet paper when a light inside the house turns on. Without saying anything, the four girls and the middle boy child grab the duffel bag and start sprinting for home. Tweedledee and I keep pace with them, although I'm still trying to figure out what kind of party that was.

Once we're out of sight of the toilet paper, the people slow to a walk and congratulate each other on the great job they did.

"Did you see how everything was covered in toilet paper?" one of the girls asks the others.

"Yeah," another says. "He's gonna be so mad when he has to clean that up tomorrow." The girls melt into giggling, and even the middle boy child laughs. They are unaware of the German Shepherds following us.

"I still know the way to Gramma's from here," Tweedledee tells me.

"I count two German Shepherds tracking and watching us," I say. "One of them, I bet, is still guarding the border, and who knows what the fourth one is up to." We have to make our break soon and leave the safety of the people. Then we must evade the German Shepherds so that we can visit Gramma without their knowledge. We reach another side road, and Tweedledee says, "This is where we need to turn right."

"Continue with me and the people," I say. "When I say, 'Now,' then you stick with me and we run as fast as we can. We must not get separated, you must stay with me. We must go as fast as we can."

I look at Tweedledee, and the playfulness she exhibited with the toilet paper minutes ago is gone. She has grown out of being a kitten in the last five minutes. She understands that if we can't shake the German Shepherds off our tails, then we may "disappear" into the Emperor's domain, and she will never see Gramma again.

"If something happens to me, make sure you get this package to Gramma," I say. "But don't worry. Nothing will happen to me."

The people continue back to my house as they chat about their toilet paper triumph, and I slow my pace so that they begin to drift further ahead of me and Tweedledee. On the next road, I turn left, and I can feel the German Shepherds closing in. We are perilously close to being outside the protection of the people.

"Princess?" Tweedledee says to me as if I don't realize the danger.

"Stick with me and trust me," I say.

"We had to take a right turn back there," Tweedledee says with a quivering voice. I continue, and Tweedledee follows me for a few steps, but then she freezes. I am alone, and I see Tweedledee alone in the middle of the road.

A bush rustles as a German Shepherd must be getting into his final position.

I sure hope my plan works.

"Now!" I yell as I sprint to Tweedledee's position and then past her. It takes Tweedledee a second to unfreeze, but she bolts with me back the way we came.

At the exact same time, two German Shepherds leap out at me.

But the skunk I had met earlier today also comes out of the bushes between us and the dogs. Before the German Shepherds can react, the skunk sprays his noxious order directly in both of their faces. As I race away with Tweedledee to Gramma's house, howls of pain ring out from the two German Shepherds.

"You see, kid," I tell Tweedledee minutes later, "Stay with me, and everything will be all right."

"That is how to lose some German Shepherds," Tweedledee says triumphantly. I'm sure the people were close enough to hear and smell the commotion, but they probably ran home. We soon arrive at Gramma's home. She will be my next ally in the struggle against the Emperor.

TWEEDLEDEE LEADS me through a cat door into Gramma's garage.

"Gramma? Gramma?" Tweedledee calls out.

Just a few seconds later, an answer comes. It's the resonant and warm voice of a grandmother who has not much else left to live for but to spoil her grandchildren.

"Is that you, Dee?"

"Gramma," Tweedledee says, "I brought a friend I want you

to meet." Tweedledee gives me a sidelong glance. I don't take kindly to being called a friend by my subjects. That is a topic we need to talk about at a different time. The garage is dark, and Gramma is obscured within a cardboard box on its side.

"Oh, wonderful," Gramma says. "What does your friend like to do? Does she like to play with string? Does she like to catch birds? Oh, let me guess: she likes to chase her tail like a dog, doesn't she?" Gramma lets out a soft chuckle as she laughs at her own joke.

"I beg your pardon, ma'am," I say, "but I am a different kind of friend to your beloved Tweedledee. My name is Princess, and I am the ruler of the domain in which she lives. My dominion consists of Rover Boulevard on the opposite side of Grand Canyon Drive. Perhaps you've heard of me. I am the one who slayed Snarl, the wicked coyote."

"Oh, I've been around long enough to hear plenty of things like that," Gramma says nonchalantly. "So why did you come to meet dear old Gramma?"

"I come here," I say, "not only on my behalf, but on behalf of my whole domain, which includes Tweedledee. My domain is under threat by one who is called the Emperor."

"Oh, now, I have heard of the Emperor. I have heard of him..."

"We have much to discuss—"

"Let me tell you about the Emperor, young lady," Gramma says as she comes out from the shadow of her cardboard box. I notice something about Gramma. She is looking in my direction, but she is not looking at me. She doesn't make eye contact with me. She can't make eye contact. Gramma is blind.

When I look at Gramma, it is as if I am looking into a magical mirror that shows me the future. Gramma is simply an older version of me. She's a gray tabby, and her fur has turned slightly scruffier, is tinged with more white hair, and she is heavier set. I, however, have my eyesight, but Gramma is blind.

"I can tell by the way you talk that you are just like I used to be," Gramma says. "There was a time when I was in charge, and everybody had to serve and honor me. But those were the days before the Empire and the Emperor."

"How old are you?" I ask.

"When I came here, there weren't that many houses yet. My domain was small, and we had to fight off coyotes ferociously on the border. There was much more wilderness. Who's the oldest cat that you know?"

I need a few seconds to think about that. I think I'm the oldest cat I know, except for...

"Patches," I say, "but he left a while ago."

Gramma's blank eyes stare off into space, and she says, "Sweet little Patches. He was a nice kitten, but there was something wrong about him that I could never quite put my paw on. You have the potential to become a great ruler, but we can discuss that another time. But this Emperor is older than me. He is an ancient foe."

That makes sense from what I know. Talking birds like the Emperor can live for decades, even outliving their owners. There are instances when they are passed from one generation to the next.

"Tell me your story," I say. I sense that this old woman wants to be heard before she will be willing to help me. "Tell me how you came to your present state."

"That's wise of you," Gramma replies. "Our history is what makes us who we are today and gives our lives meaning. We can't afford to forget our past, or we die—figuratively, and literally."

I nod, and Gramma continues.

"I had solidified my kingdom, but people constantly built new houses. New houses brought new enemies. One day, the Emperor moved nearby. To make a long story short, he worked with dogs, some of whom were much larger and more powerful than me. Without the Emperor, I could easily control those foolish dogs, but there's something about the combination of those dogs and the Emperor that made for a dangerous mix. I was once trapped by the Emperor and his dogs, and I couldn't fight them all off. I don't know how many dogs I sent to the veterinarian. One brave dog even came and tried to rescue me. He lost his life trying to rescue me. I fought valiantly. But, in the end, the dogs held me down, and the Emperor came and scratched up my face and blinded me. I was left for dead.

"My people found me and rushed me to the vet. Obviously, I lived, but I could no longer see. Time passed, but I don't know how much. I felt that I preferred death to humiliation and blindness. I spent much of my days indoors to regain my strength, but I had no purpose. I felt bad about the dog who died trying to rescue me. When I finally ventured out, I did so in hopes that the Emperor, or his dogs, would finally finish me off. I had nothing to live for. The Emperor, however, had different ideas."

Gramma needs to get to the point.

"Instead of ending my life, the Emperor would let me live, but I had to be his puppet for the rest of my life. I didn't care about my own life, so he threatened the lives of my children and future grandchildren. I would have to do his bidding for them to stay alive. I would have to do tasks and errands for him."

"What sort of tasks?" I ask.

"To my surprise, I hardly had to do anything. Again, much time passed, and I'm not sure how much. I honestly wanted my life to end. But then, I had not only my own offspring, but I also had grandchildren. I have many grandchildren, and a few of them would visit me, but now only one comes to visit. It wasn't too long ago that the Emperor came to me with one of his tasks. He periodically gives me catnip. He told me I would have to deliver that to Dee, and then Dee would have to put it in a certain garage at a certain location."

"Didn't you ask why?"

"You don't question the Emperor. It's a sign of insubordination."

"How could you have lived so long? Like you, I would've preferred death over defeat to the Emperor."

"I suppose you find other things to live for," Gramma says with a slight smile as her blank eyes look up to the sky. "You discover that what you live for isn't often worth dying for. If I didn't handle the catnip, then Dee would never be allowed to visit me again. Then I certainly would die."

Tweedledee interrupts the conversation and says, "You can come live with us, Gramma!"

"Oh, that would be wonderful." Gramma chuckles. "I just don't think I could. I'm so old."

"We will defeat the Emperor," Tweedledee continues, "and you can come live in Princess' domain."

I'm dumbfounded, but I need help, and so I have little choice but to make a promise.

"We can get you out of here to Tweedledee in my domain," I

say. "You could see Tweedledee every day. But first we need to defeat the Emperor. To do that, you just have to do one simple thing for me."

Gramma doesn't agree, but she doesn't stop me either, so I continue.

"The next time catnip is given to you, give this tiny package to the cat who delivers it."

I push the package I've been carrying this whole evening over to her. It contains the miniature tape recorder that I took from my people's children. "It's better if you don't know what's in it." Gramma doesn't say anything. She smiles as she uses her front paw to feel for the package and slide it towards herself.

"If anybody asks," I say, "we were never here. Tweedledee, you can go home safely. You have orders for safe passage."

"What about you?" Tweedledee asks.

"I will need to find my own way across the Wall."

7

I watch from a distance as Tweedledee crosses the Wall to safety. I also spot an onlooking German Shepherd, but I don't think Tweedledee notices. She's nervous, not confident she still has safe passage. I relax slightly once Tweedledee passes out of the Emperor's domain safely.

I have not figured out how I will leave. The skunk temporarily disabled two German Shepherds. Another German Shepherd guards the Wall. The fourth German Shepherd, no doubt, is hunting for me. If I am to take advantage of the two disabled German Shepherds, I need to cross the Wall tonight.

The German Shepherds must expect this. Since they are doing all that they can to guard the border, I decide this is a perfect chance to do something they don't expect. I go away from Grand Canyon Drive, deeper into the Emperor's territory, towards the old gas station. This will give me an opportunity to gather intelligence.

Ten minutes later, I arrive at the old, abandoned gas station. A newer one across the street and down the road a bit gets all the business. This one was shut down years ago. A thick yellow tape, like a ribbon, encircles the old gas station. The letters, "CONDEMNED BY E.P.A.," are written on the tape to warn people away.

I enter anyways.

Inside, the old gas station is vacant. Empty metal shelves line the perimeter of the convenience store, and a counter is in the corner where the cash register must have sat. Surprisingly, the ceiling and roof are mostly missing. Wind-storms must have torn it off. Dust has blown in, coating everything with a fine layer of dirt.

I think I recall my people discussing this old gas station and the E.P.A. a few months ago. E.P.A. means "Environmental Protection Agency." Apparently, this gas station had been illegally and profusely leaking gas onto the ground, endangering the environment and precious animals like me. The E.P.A. accordingly shut this gas station down.

From inside, I see that the almighty Animal Control building is nearby. Like a moth drawn to light, I slink over to Animal Control. As I sit next to the window, I overhear their telephone conversations.

Most of the telephone calls I hear are just like others: "Okay, ma'am, okay. I know, right?" and so on. There's a break in the phone conversations when two of the Animal Control workers have a discussion. One of them is going to be driving the vehicle away for a while. Perhaps this is my chance to ride on the Animal Control vehicle back to my domain. What wonderful irony that would be. The same Animal Control vehicle that means the end for so many animals would be my salvation. But then they say that they're taking the Animal Control vehicle to put an animal to sleep.

One of them says, "I hate to say it, but I won't be sad when it's time to put that monster dog to sleep in a few days. That thing is a beast."

That must be the dog they captured on Thanksgiving.

Because of the Animal Control vehicle's destination, I decide against trying to ride it. I want to explore the town more, especially the grocery store.

Before I go, an Animal Control employee has a phone conversation that could aid me against the Emperor.

I don't know what the caller is saying, but the Animal Control employee assures them that German Shepherds typically are not dangerous. The Animal Control employee seems a bit defensive, and he tells the person on the other end that if the German Shepherd has tags and remains on the owner's private property, there's nothing to be done.

I smile to myself.

I like to think that I have frustrated these German Shepherds enough that people notice their agitation. When the Animal Control vehicle pulls away, the remaining employee lays his head on the desk and takes a nap.

The grocery store, where my people go to get food, and the pizza delivery shop, where the oldest girl child ordered pizza the other night, is nearby. As I walk to the pizza delivery shop, I realize what feels so strange on this side of the Wall. There are no stray animals. There are no homeless or disabled. Everything seems just a little bit too clinical.

I remember my idea of catching a ride with the pizza delivery boy earlier, and I think that is my best chance to get back home. I will have to hide on the roof until lunchtime the next day, when people call in their pizza orders. One night out in the cold is enough for me. I then lay by the window to over-hear where the cars are going, but none are going near my house.

I listen for hours, and the sun begins to set. It's getting colder, and the German Shepherds howl in the distance. They must be at full strength now, probably ferociously guarding the border. I wonder when they will start searching for me elsewhere.

I continue to wait, hoping to hear an address near my home. Finally, on what seems like the last order of the night, I recog-nize the address for the pizza delivery. I recognize the address because it's the Emperor's new house, my neighbor.

Almost as ironic as being saved by the Animal Control van.

I wait in a bush near the backseat of the delivery car. I've learned the delivery boy's routine. All I have to do is hop in the back of his car without him noticing.

I'm only feet away, under a bush, but the delivery boy changes his routine. He only has a single pizza, and instead of putting it on the backseat, he puts it on the front passenger seat. Before I come up with a new plan, he backs up and leaves me stranded.

I climb up onto the roof of the pizza delivery shop, and I spend another night shivering and hungry, listening to the howls of the German Shepherds.

I sleep fitfully at night. I will try the pizza delivery again, and I won't be picky about the address. However, people don't order pizza in the morning, so I have time to explore. Behind the pizza shop, I find an opening to the sewer. A manhole cover wasn't replaced correctly. Are there underground tunnels that could take me across—under—the Wall? Perhaps I can explore these tunnels and find my way back to my territory. Maybe with sewer tunnels I can move freely across the Wall without the Emperor or his German Shepherds knowing.

I stick my head in, but the stench warns me away. What is that horrible odor, and what are those noises? I suspect that is where all the homeless and derelict go to hide, driven underground into the sewers. If I went down there, I would be eaten alive by whatever the Emperor drove underground—if I didn't die from the stench first.

That night, my multiple unsuccessful attempts to go with the pizza delivery boy discourage me. The delivery boy catches me one time and kicks me in the ribs before I can get into his backseat. I sit on top of the pizza delivery shop, shivering, wondering if I will die here. Perhaps garbage trucks could take me across the Wall, but trash day isn't for several days, after Christmas. I don't know how many more days I can survive here on my own. I'm desperately hungry, constantly cold to my core, and I'm not sure I can think straight anymore.

Another night passes, and I'm still lying low, hiding from the Emperor's agents. I'm at the end of my rope. If I remember correctly, today is Christmas Eve. If I am going to survive another day to face the Emperor, I'm going to need a Christmas miracle to save me.

ONLY ON CHRISTMAS EVE do most people gather at a place they call "church" at night. Christmas is such a wonderful holiday for most people, but this Christmas Eve is the Christmas Eve that I give up. I'm hungry, I'm cold, and now I'm getting wet. I don't care if the German Shepherds find me. I trudge along the sidewalk towards the Wall as the snow falls on me lightly. It started as a dusting, but it falls harder the closer I get to the Wall. I let the snowflakes build up on my fur and then melt. I don't bother to shake them off.

I go past one church, and I can hear them singing a popular song: "Silent Night." It is indeed a silent night. It may be the night my domain loses me as their empress. I plod onward, hoping that the German Shepherds find me to end my misery. The odds of the German Shepherds capturing me grow exponentially with each step, but they don't come.

Has the Emperor given them new orders, or am I incredibly lucky?

I pass another church, but their Christmas Eve service is over, and cars are slowly leaving the parking lot. At first, I assume they are driving slowly because of the fresh snow that is still falling, but as I go past the church, I also see that many cars are driving slowly simply so that they can observe the beautiful Christmas decorations people have put on their houses. Perhaps my lack of food is going to my head, but I have to admit that the Christmas lights and snow are strangely beautiful on a silent night.

Several cars crawl past me, and I get a painfully obvious idea. The cars are going so slowly, I can hop on top of one and simply ride it to my new territory. My territory is on Rover Boulevard, a main thoroughfare of town, and there's no reason to think that some of these cars will not continue past my house.

I shake off the wet snow and look around warily. I hope that I have not been too carefree, even hoping that the German Shepherds would capture me, just as I find a narrow means of escape. They don't come, though.

A car loaded with children leaves the church parking lot. I figure it is just the type of car that would go to look at Christmas lights, and so I wait on the edge of the road for it to creep by. It passes me, and I run after it.

This is the most dog-like behavior I have ever engaged in.

I jump onto the top of the car when it sits at a stop sign for a second. Under normal circumstances, I can't ride on top of a car like this, but with snowy roads and everybody gazing at Christmas decorations, I can nearly relax.

I look ahead, and the Wall, Grand Canyon Drive, approaches. As expected, one German Shepherd stands guard at the border. There's no way a German Shepherd would dare to attack a car. That would land those German Shepherds in Animal Control's pound for sure.

A sharp howl breaks through the cold and silent night behind me. It's followed by several vicious barks. They grow louder as the barking dog comes closer. The German Shepherd standing guard at the border has latched his eyes onto the vehicle I'm riding. More barking joins the chorus, and they come right up to the car when we reach the Wall. The car stops at a stop sign, and I look down from the car at the four German Shepherds barking wildly next to the car. The car inches forward to go across the border into my own territory, and one of the German Shepherds makes a bold gamble. He walks directly in front of the car and bares his fangs at the car. He knows that the people would dare not run over a dog.

Honk!

The driver person presses the horn repeatedly to scare the German Shepherd away. It doesn't work. I'm afraid the people may decide to make a sharp turn and drive quickly, flinging me off the roof. Then I would be left for the German Shepherds.

The car creeps forward slowly, inch by inch. The German Shepherd stands his ground, but the car continues slowly. Finally, the German Shepherd moves out of the way just as the car presses against him. The car speeds up slightly. The driver is probably relieved to be away from those crazy dogs. He is nowhere near as relieved as I am.

The car slows back down once we are across the Wall, and I look back to see four German Shepherds pacing in anger. One of them has his tail between his legs, probably ashamed of what he will have to report to the Emperor.

To my relief, the car continues down Rover Boulevard towards my house, and I feel warmth returning to my body. I have been without hope for a long time, and I'm just now beginning to ponder what I will do now that I am still alive and back in my territory.

As the car passes my house, I see that my people have decorated it. The car slows down to marvel, and this is my chance. I hop down onto the back bumper, and then into my front yard. I straggle to my front door and I collapse. I can't go another inch.

I do something I thought I would never do.

Meow!? Meow!?

I let out the same pathetic meow that Max does. It is my best imitation of him. It always draws the attention of my people. I only have enough energy to let it out a few times. I'm so exhausted.

A car pulls into my driveway, and the bright lights from the car wake me up. My people have come home. The children pile out of the car.

"Kimberly Lane always has the best Christmas lights on Christmas Eve," the oldest girl child says.

"Ugh," the middle boy child says. "I just want to go to sleep so Christmas morning gets here faster."

"I'm never going to go to sleep," the youngest girl child says. "I will stay up all night to see if Santa is real."

"Dad is the one who eats the cookies you put out for him," the middle boy child says.

"Who thinks I would eat the cookies?" the big man person says.

Then, they see me.

"It's Princess!" the oldest girl child yells as they reach the front door.

The big man person scoops me up, the big woman person unlocks the front door, and they carry me in. The next few minutes are muddled in my mind. They dry me with a towel, give me water, but then the whir of the can opener brings me to life. My eyes open, and I feel a rumble in my belly. I then scarf down I don't know how much canned cat food, but I feel like I'm about to throw up because I ate so much so quickly. I wash it down with water, and then the people wrap me in a warm towel that must've been on a heater. It is cozy warm. They set me down on the couch near the lit up Christmas tree so I can rest. The children coddle me, and I blush at the thought of Max seeing me like this.

To my relief, my people don't put me outside this night. It's a special Christmas Eve for me. I fall asleep on the couch. I'm not sure how long I sleep. It feels like days. When I wake up, I still can't believe that I am alive, out of the Emperor's territory, and still in the fight against him.

I look about the room, and the Christmas tree is still lit up, but now the Christmas lights reflect off shiny wrapping paper, bright bows, and gifts that fill the room. I must have slept through Santa's visit.

The children are excited, counting their gifts to see who got the most. I need to prepare to see Max when they let him in. He can't see me as a coddled and weak kitten. He must see me as his empress.

"I'm so glad Princess is back," the youngest girl says.

"Me too," the middle boy child says. That's about the most affection I would expect out of him.

"Me too," the oldest girl child says, "but I'm still sad that Max is gone."

"I'll bet Max went looking for Princess," the youngest girl says.

Max is gone? When? How?

8

"There's nothing we can do about Max right now," the big man person says to the youngest girl child. "Don't let it ruin Christmas morning. I promise to call Animal Control tomorrow, but they're closed on Christmas Day."

This lifts the youngest girl's spirits, and she joins her siblings by the Christmas tree, eager to open the gifts.

I watch as everybody takes turns opening their gifts. The oldest girl child gets several pop music cassette tapes. The son gets several toys that don't make sense to me, but also gets a miniature train set. The youngest girl child gets many stuffed animals, including stuffed dogs. Honestly, that's a little bizarre to me. It's not as if I have stuffed people to play with.

Max's absence puts a damper on the morning for the children. If Max were here, he would play with the balled up and discarded wrapping paper. He would be entranced by the new toys, noises and sounds, and he would just make the whole event overall a little bit more fun. Also, without him here, I don't have anybody to boss around.

Once the kids have opened all their gifts, they give their mother and father a big hug, and they run to their rooms to play with their new toys.

I go outside and call Tweedledee. It's time we have another emergency Cat Council. She grudgingly agrees to attend.

"The first matter of business," I say to Tweedledee to start the emergency Cat Council, "is that New Year's Eve and my meeting with the Emperor is less than a week away. We must defeat those German Shepherds beforehand, or the meeting will be a disaster for freedom lovers everywhere. We must get Max back. Surely it's not a coincidence that he is missing."

"It is not a coincidence," Tweedledee says. "Animal Control got him. But it's not just Animal Control. A German Shepherd came into your domain while you were gone."

This has my attention.

"The German Shepherd got between Max and your house. Max couldn't get back home. The German Shepherd chased Max, and Max climbed a tree. He avoided him as best as he could, but the German Shepherd was making quite the commotion. Eventually, somebody must've heard the noise and called Animal Control. The German Shepherd has a collar and tags, and so Animal Control probably just took the German Shepherd back to his home. But Max, he—"

"Doesn't have tags," I say to finish Tweedledee's thought.

I don't allow cats in my territory to have tags or bells on their collars. All they do is attract predators. In this instance it worked against Max. If Max had been wearing tags, Animal Control would've taken him back to my house. Instead, Animal Control has taken Max to the pound in the Emperor's territory.

Animal Control probably brought Max in when I was trying to escape in a pizza delivery car.

"I hope the Emperor does not have agents inside the Animal Control pound. My people will call Animal Control first thing tomorrow. If all goes well, they should bring Max home tomorrow. Also, we should receive another message from our mole inside the Emperor's territory. This will have vital information that determines our next actions. I intend to enlist more help from Jacques, the freedom fighter. We will need his help if we are going to defeat the Emperor and free Fluffy, assuming our people can release Max from Animal Control tomorrow."

I adjourn the Council and go back into my house. I find a nice sunbeam to rest in. I need time to think and ponder. I also need time to rest and sleep after my three days of being trapped in the Emperor's territory.

I sleep soundly until my rest is interrupted by the Christmas dinner. My people get together for holidays with friends and neighbors. Thankfully, pets are not invited to this Christmas dinner.

Chad comes over with his parents, and he brings his favorite new toys from Christmas. The children show off their new toys and play with them together.

"You won't believe what Chad really wants for Christmas," Chad's mom says to my big woman person. "Chad desperately wants a dog, especially now that Tweedledum is gone. He feels we need to replace him. I don't know if Chad will be able to take care of a dog, though. Cats clean themselves, and they can feed themselves if they need to. Dogs need to be walked, groomed, fed, and I just don't know if Chad is ready for that kind of responsibility."

This woman has a real head on her shoulders. It doesn't take a genius to see that dogs are horrible pets, in my not so humble opinion.

"I might go to Animal Control tomorrow," my big man person says. "We're hoping Max is there. He's been missing. I could let you know what animals they have there for adoption."

"That's a great idea," Chad's mom says. "That way, I don't have to take him there and have him fixate on the one animal that he wants."

"Maybe we need a new dog, too. We—" Chief's owner says, but a discrete jab from his wife stops him. He recovers and continues, "We have been housing the new neighbors' parrot at our house since they left for a Christmas vacation, and it reminds me how much I prefer dogs."

The Emperor is now in Chief's house? And Chad wants a pet dog?

I must take action. If Chad were to own a dog, the Emperor would certainly take control of it. I need to go talk to Chief and ask him to do a big favor for me. Really, it's not a favor for me. It is now a vital part of defeating the Emperor.

I leave before I see what happens when Chief's owner drinks too much eggnog again.

EARLY THE NEXT MORNING, the day after Christmas, I hop up onto the fence overlooking Chief's pen. Unlike most times, I'm not here for advice. I'm here for the plan we made last night. He will do a horrible deed. And yet, it is a necessary deed. I unfasten the latch to his pen. I hurry to Tweedledee's yard, and I unlatch her fence as well. I come back to Chief, and I knock softly on the side of his doghouse.

"Wake up, Chief," I say. "It's time for you to do your worst. I'm sorry you have to do this, but there's no other way."

A whimper escapes from the doghouse.

"I said I'm sorry," I say. "You know that if there was any other way, we would do that. But I don't think there is." I hear some rustling from inside the doghouse, and Chief sticks his head out.

"Everybody is going to be so mad at me, even my master," Chief says. "I wish I could tell him I'm sorry right now."

"People don't understand what needs to be done in this world," I say. "If people understood what was really necessary, they would be the ones running this world."

And us cats wouldn't be running the world, I shudder to think.

"Do your best, or worst, as it is," I say as Chief slowly pads out of his pen and makes his way over to Tweedledee's yard.

I'm curious to see what Chief does. He walks with a hitch because of his arthritis, and I'm wondering if he has the strength and energy to do what he needs to do. A transfiguration occurs before my eyes. Somehow, Chief channels the energy to become like a puppy, if only for half a minute. He tears around Tweedledee's yard, chewing everything in sight. He knocks everything over that is not fastened to the ground, and he lifts his leg by the back door and pees on it. Anything that is not made out of metal goes through the meat grinder that his jaws are. Chief rushes to the front yard, grabs the people's trash from the curb, and he hauls one of the bags back to the backyard. It leaves a trail of trash. His chest heaves from exertion, and he's nearly at his end. I know, however, he's truly at his end when he squats and plants a giant poop on the back door step.

Chief wanders slowly back to his own pen. We leave both

gates open so everybody will know that Chief, a dog, is to blame. Once Chief is back inside his doghouse, I say, "I'm sorry, again."

"It's okay," comes the resigned response. "It was fun for a few seconds." I can't stick around to commiserate with Chief for the punishment he is sure to receive because I hear the garbage truck approaching.

I rush out to my front yard where my big man person has already placed all of the Christmas trash on the curb. I watch with eagerness as the garbage truck pulls up, and I notice a small chalk mark above the front wheel. It's a mark that has been placed there by the mole.

When the truck stops and starts gathering the trash from my curb, I hop up to a small compartment in between the driver's cab and the large trash bin in the back. Just as the mole said, there is an empty can of cat food. In this case, there are several of them. I knock them all onto the street. I watch the garbage truck rumble away, taking away my people's Christmas refuse. I shuttle the empty cans into my garage one at a time, eager to see what's inside. I empty them out, and they all contain the same thing. They are full of flyers advertising the adoption of cats from Animal Control.

I race over to the rabbit family who lives near my backyard and ask them to spread these flyers throughout the neighborhood. The rabbits are eager to help, and they enlist other animals to help as well. Ever since I saved this rabbit family from Snarl the coyote, they have been willing to do almost anything I tell them.

By the time the animals have dispersed the flyers, the people in my house are starting to wake up. Inside my house, it's oddly quiet without Max. As much as he drives me crazy and bothers me, things do seem a bit empty without him. The younger two children play with their new Christmas toys, but the oldest girl child is not passing up a chance to sleep until at least noon. It's funny how teenagers are apparently like cats in some ways. Imagine if teenagers ruled the world.

"Is it time yet, Daddy?" the youngest girl child asks when I see them eating breakfast.

"Animal Control doesn't open until eight," the big man person says. "I will call then. I promise. Please do not ask again."

The youngest girl child instead asks every five minutes, and the big man person simply says, "What did I tell you before?"

When 8 AM arrives, the younger two children gather by the telephone in the kitchen as the big man person calls Animal Control.

"I'm calling about my missing cat," the big man person says. "I'm hoping that you have picked him up... Okay, well, he has long fur, mostly orange, except he has white feet and a white dot on his back. I would also say that he's not very smart, he's very playful, and he has a very loud and obnoxious meow that almost sounds like he's begging."

This big man person is quite astute, in my opinion.

After a few seconds, the big man person's eyes enlarge, and the children see it, too, because their faces light up in anticipation of what Animal Control is saying on the other end of the telephone.

"You do have him?" the big man person says just as much of an exclamation as a question.

But then as the big man person listens, his brow furls, and a concerned look spreads across his face. The children mirror his concern.

"Somebody called asking about Max before, and they want him put to sleep?" the big man person asks. He must hear an affirmative response come from Animal Control, and the big man person says, "No, certainly do not put Max to sleep. Who would've called and said such a thing?"

I know exactly who would've gotten on the telephone and told Animal Control to kill an innocent, though foolish, cat.

"We'll be there in just a few minutes to pick him up," the big man person says, and then he hangs up the phone. "Come on, let's go get Max!" The two younger children cheer in unison, and they go get in the car still wearing their pajamas.

I hope they get there in time!

Just as I see the big man person drive away with the two younger children in his car to rescue Max, I hear a shriek from Tweedledee's backyard. Seconds later, Chief's owner starts yelling at Chief. Apparently, lots of eggnog doesn't prevent him from waking up at eight in the morning. Chief's owner chastises him harshly for the mess he made.

I go outside to Chief's pen, and Chief's owner is red in the face, saying a whole bunch of words that sound very nasty, even though I'm not exactly sure what they mean. He's threatening to do lots of crazy things to Chief for what he did in Twee-dledee's yard. Eventually, the tirade dies down, and the man goes back into his house, no doubt to drink some eggnog. Chief looks up at me sadly from down in his pen. I say the only thing that I can: "Thanks."

"It's okay," Chief says. "I can barely hear him anyways because my ears don't work well."

I go to Tweedledee's backyard to look at it again, and I am still in awe at the mess that Chief made inside this yard. It looks like a pooping tornado passed through.

But then I hear the very thing that makes it all worth it. Chad's mom yells to Chad: "We are *never* getting a pet dog if this is what a dog is like!" She holds up the flyer advertising the adoption of cats and declares, "We will get a cat!"

I just hope Chief's owner decides to keep Chief.

"THAT DOG IS OLD," Chief's owner says from Tweedledee's backyard. "I think it's about time we put him to sleep and put him out of his misery. He's clearly going crazy, acting like this." Chief's owner, recovered from eggnog, has hurried into Tweedledee's backyard in his pajamas to help clean up the mess, embarrassed by the way his dog behaved.

"I would like to get a smaller dog," the man's wife says as she watches her husband pick up Chief's poop with plastic bags. "I always said those big dogs were not worth the trouble." The man grunts, tired of being told, "See, I told you so," by his wife.

These statements deepen my regret for asking Chief to make this mess. Chief's actions put his own life in danger. I figured his owners would chastise him, punish him, or withhold doggy treats. It never occurred to me that they might decide he's old and senile, and therefore needs to be put to sleep. I want to tell Chief I'm sorry again, but saying it again won't do any good. What kind of empress am I if I have to force others in my domain to sacrifice themselves?

The grinding noise of the garage door opener cuts my musings short. It signals that my people will arrive in their car very soon. I rush to the front yard, and once the car stops in the driveway, the door swings open, and the two younger children triumphantly pull out the cat carrier. Max is indeed inside of it.

I rush into the garage ahead of the car, and I run into the house so that I can see Max.

"I guess I can get up before lunch," the oldest girl child says with a grin as she makes her way into the family room, apparently awoken by all the commotion.

"Max!" The kids cheer in unison as they release Max. He gleefully stumbles out of the cat carrier. He has a little bit less fur, but he certainly doesn't look like he's lost his mind or been abused or neglected.

"They told me I called just in time this morning," the big man person says to the big woman person. "They were about to load him up in the van to take him to put him to sleep. I can't imagine who or why anybody would call to specifically say that Max had to be put to sleep."

"I wonder," the big woman person says. "At least he's home safe now, but I wonder what Princess thinks of all this."

A year ago, I would've been celebrating Max's potential demise, but now, I'm excited Max is home. Getting Max back safely is a victory against the Emperor. He must have called Animal Control and talked with a person's voice to tell them to put Max to sleep.

Once all the people are done fawning over Max, I need to ask him everything he knows about Animal Control.

"Good to see you, Princess," Max says with a grin.

"I know, I know," I say. "I'm so happy to see you, we could exchange hugs, *blah blah blah*, but you need to tell me anything you can about Animal Control that can help us against the Emperor. We've got work to do."

"Okay. Well, Animal Control was actually pretty boring. I was in this wire cage. I was the only animal in my room. There was another room, and I'm not sure what was in there. The

Animal Control workers were very careful with whatever was in there. I have a feeling it was some kind of crazy attack dog, but I don't know. Maybe somebody had a pet tiger they had to take away. I did hear the Animal Control people talk about me, though. They said somebody called and claimed that I would pee uncontrollably all the time. Don't get me wrong, I do enjoy a good bathroom break, but I can certainly control it. They were talking about how they were going to have to put me in a van, drive me away, and then put me to sleep. I wasn't sure I wanted to go, so I made sure to sleep as much as I could."

Max obviously doesn't understand that Animal Control meant that they were going to kill him, not just help him sleep.

"That's all?" I ask. "If you think of anything else, make sure you tell me. It could be crucial for us to defeat the Emperor. It's time for another emergency Cat Council. Let's go get Tweedledee." Max reluctantly follows me outside.

"Not another meeting," Tweedledee says with a roll of her eyes. "That's all we ever do. Meetings, meetings, meetings..."

However, we don't have a chance to have an emergency Cat Council. Chief's owner is still cleaning up Tweedledee's backyard, and Chad halfheartedly helps. As planned, he is less excited about the possibility of getting his own dog. Chad's parents arrive home with a surprise for him.

"Chad!" his mom calls from the house. "Come on in. We've got something special to show you." Max, Tweedledee and I follow Chad to his house. Through the sliding glass door, we watch Chad's parents open an animal carrier. A cat steps out. I recognize the cat.

It's Fluffy, the mole's brother. He's the cat I saw the German Shepherd catch as he crossed the Wall, Grand Canyon Drive.

Now that the mole's brother is safe, the mole can defect to my territory without fear of the Emperor harming Fluffy.

The Emperor's empire is weakening, and there remains more of my plan to unfold.

"FIRST OF ALL," I begin in the Cat Council, "I would like to welcome our newest member to the Cat Council: Fluffy." I clap my paws to show my appreciation, and Max and Tweedledee join me. "Of course, welcome back to Max, too. We are thrilled to have you back. Much has changed over the last few weeks, and we are at a crucial time. This is a crucial time for the whole animal kingdom, people everywhere, and for all of history. We are on a precipice, looking into a dark abyss. If we are not victorious, we, and the rest of the world, will sink into that abyss." Max, Tweedledee, and Fluffy seem more confused than impressed with my speech. I have to make it crystal clear for them.

"We must attack now. Now is the time that we make a full on frontal assault. The Emperor is temporarily living in Chief's owner's house. We will dethrone him. We will cut the head off the snake, and the rest of the snake will die."

Fluffy crouches down and covers his eyes with his paws and says, "No! He'll know we're coming somehow! He'll trap me again, and then..."

"Attacking isn't really my thing," Tweedledee says with disinterest.

"Didn't you try that before," Max asks, "and the Emperor sent you running?"

"There are four of us!" I say with a booming voice. "Who

can climb and leap with the agility of a cougar? Who could bite the head off a rat, and who can scratch like a whole package of razor blades?"

"You don't mean us, do you?" Max asks.

"Of course I mean us!" I say. "We were put on this planet with a destiny, a purpose. We are to keep people in their proper functions and roles, but an overgrown blabbermouth bird has temporarily threatened the balance of power. Everything was peaceful. I fear we were distracted by these jolly holidays."

"Don't underestimate the Emperor," Fluffy says. "I've stood against him, and—"

"Now all four of us will not only stand, but we will strike out and defeat them."

"I'm not much of a fighter," Tweedledee says.

"Max was not much of a fighter either," I say, "but he has become an elite warrior."

This is true; on our previous adventure to Uncle Bill's farm, Max was forced through a brutal military boot camp, and he did become an elite warrior. He keeps that secret from everybody else now.

"Stick with me," Max says to Tweedledee. "We will do okay as a team. I promise."

"And now," I say as I look to Fluffy, "is the time for you, Fluffy, to gain justice. Now is the time to right the wrongs that the Emperor has perpetrated by imprisoning you unjustly, and then using you against your very own brother. We will defeat him and set the captives free. The oppressed will see daylight again as the prison doors swing open. We do this now; save your brother now."

"Okay," Fluffy says. "For my brother. His name is Karl, by the way."

"You all in?" I say as more of a command than a question. They all nod.

"We attack at night. When Chief's owner goes in and out of his house, I'll wedge the door open slightly so that we can enter later, surveil the house, and then close in on the Emperor's room. We will end his reign of terror."

I adjourn the Council meeting, and the other cats leave to get rested and to prepare for tonight's assault on the Emperor.

Hours later, I sneak in behind Chief's owner as he enters his house from the garage. I stick some old bubble gum from my children people in the lock so that it doesn't latch completely. We will be able to sneak in tonight with ease as the Emperor sleeps. I don't even tell Chief what we are going to do. I can't risk any of the Emperor's agents overhearing the plan.

When we all meet late at night, oh-one-hundred hour, to prepare for the assault, I barely recognize the three cats.

"We have camouflage," Max announces. All three of them have what appears to be dirt and ash rubbed all over. "We took charcoal from Tweedledee's people's grill. We aren't all gray tabbies like you," Max explains. "This dark coal will make us invisible to the Emperor in the dark house."

"Excellent," I say to commend Max. The four of us, under the cover of dark, slink our way towards Chief and the Emperor's house. We are an elite unit of spies, and Max leads the assault that will end the Emperor and restore freedom.

———

THE DOOR into the house from the garage is still stuck slightly open, just as I left it. Tweedledee and I will check the bedrooms and bathrooms to make sure they are clear before we attack the

Emperor in his room. Max and Fluffy will clear the kitchen and the living rooms.

We have a special code. If we encounter each other, one of us says "hair," and the other responds, "ball." That indicates we are both on the same side. If one of us says, "hair," but the response isn't, "ball," then we know it's an enemy. If things go horribly wrong, I will yell, "Litterbox!" and we will all get out of there as fast as we can. If assistance is required, we will yell, "Help!"

I am certain the Emperor is kept in a room at the far end of the house. We first have to make sure he's not somewhere else in the house.

"Everybody understand which rooms you need to clear before we attack Emperor?" I ask one last time before we spread out to search the house.

"Won't the people know that cats killed their precious bird?" Tweedledee asks. "Assuming, of course, that we succeed on this mission."

"I have something planned for later," I say. Tweedledee's question has me a little unsettled, though. The best way to overcome my nerves is to get on with the mission.

I head straight down the main hallway of the house, past the living room and kitchen. Max and Fluffy will clear those rooms. As I walk by the kitchen, I'm disgusted by how dirty the house is. I can feel a fine dust, like a powder on the floor, as I walk down the hallway.

When was the last time this house was cleaned?

Tweedledee and I approach the first bedroom. Tweedledee waits outside to cover me as I lunge in to the bedroom, and I discover that it is a relatively small bedroom with very little in it. I'm able to search it quickly, and it's clearly empty.

I'm about to meet Tweedledee in the hallway when she calls out in a raised voice, "Help!" I dash back to her, and she says, "Something is stuck to my paw... *Grrr*."

I've seen these before. They are used as mousetraps. It's a small plastic tray with a sticky substance on it. Mice get stuck to it when they walk across it. I pull it off without getting stuck myself.

Odd place to put a mousetrap.

"It's okay," I say, "now be quiet. We have another room to search."

We go down the hall several more paces, and I make Tweedledee wait in the hallway while I search this room. It's empty like the first room.

A loud crash from where we entered the house shatters the silence.

Max and Fluffy call out, "Help! Help!"

I rush down the hallway, backtracking all the way to the living room. The Christmas tree is now lit up, and it blinds me momentarily. The Christmas tree lies on its side with Max and Fluffy entangled in its branches and ornaments. Fluffy struggles to free himself from a string of Christmas lights, crunching glass ornaments in the process. Max attempts to wrangle Fluffy free from the Christmas light trap, and I hurry to unplug the string of lights.

"What in the name of the feline gods?" I ask with a sharp whisper to scold Max and Fluffy.

"It was booby-trapped," Max explains.

"Let's get out of here," Fluffy says. "I knew this was a mistake."

"No!" I say adamantly. "We've lost the element of surprise, but don't forget that there are still four of us. The booby trap was just to scare us away. What could the Emperor have that could really defeat four cats in this house?"

Nobody has a good answer to that question, and so I start walking towards the far end of the house where the Emperor must be. All three cats follow me. Once we're all gathered around the door into the Emperor's room, I remind them of the plan.

"Max will push the door open with all of his strength, and then I will rush in to go for the immediate attack. Fluffy and Tweedledee will go to the sides and attack as quickly as they can. Max will cover the escape through the door. The key is that one of us sinks our fangs into that nasty flying beast as soon as possible, and then don't let go until it's over."

"Okay," Max and Tweedledee say in unison. Fluffy nods tentatively.

I hold up my paw to indicate the countdown for Max to burst the door open.

Three...

Two...

One!

Max shoves the door open, and I rush in with my fur puffed up and my claws extended. I zoom towards the Emperor's bird-cage on its stand, and I can sense Tweedledee and Fluffy flanking me. I send the birdcage tumbling to the ground with a metallic clatter, but the Emperor isn't there. We race around, frenzied to sink our claws into the Emperor. After only a few seconds, it's clear that the Emperor is not in this room. The room is empty.

There's a second or two of silence, and then all three of the other cats look at me.

"Litterbox!" I say.

The others return a confused look.

"Get out of here!" I clarify.

The three of them rush out the room, down the hallway, and towards the garage. I follow behind them.

Seconds later, we all arrive under the lilac bush in my yard. Our hearts pound from exertion.

"What happened!?" Tweedledee asks once her breathing calms down slightly.

"The Emperor wasn't anywhere in that house," I say. "I feared it might have been some kind of trap, and so we had to abort."

"It was a trap," Fluffy says. "He knew we were coming. He was going to trap us in there, and then... who knows what?"

"If the Emperor isn't in that house," I say, "that means he's up to no good elsewhere. That's what has me worried now."

"The Emperor wants to know if his home is invaded while he's away," Max says. "If the knocked over Christmas tree doesn't tell him, and his toppled over cage doesn't tell him, then the disturbed sticky traps for mice will tell him. If that doesn't tell him, then Princess' paw prints in the flour on the kitchen floor will tell him."

I look down at my paws, and a white powder covers them— flour. My tracks were left behind at the scene of the aborted attack. The Emperor, wherever he is, will know of my failure.

9

It's much easier the next day to coax the other three cats to come with me to meet Jacques.

"It's not like we're attacking his lair," I had explained, especially to Fluffy. "He's on our side against the Emperor."

I hope.

We're on our way to meet Jacques at the landfill. This is necessary if we are going to defeat those German Shepherds, and ultimately the Emperor. Gramma previously gave a package to the mole, Karl. I need to retrieve that package. I only have four days to be ready for my meeting with the Emperor at the old gas station. This package is the key to defeating the Emperor at that meeting.

What worries me most as we travel to meet Jacques at the landfill is what the Emperor could have been up to last night.

Where was he?

"We should have reached the landfill by now, shouldn't we?"

Fluffy asks. "The Emperor still has agents out here to lead us astray or to capture us."

"We just need to correct course," Max says. The boot camp that Max went through at Uncle Bill's farm is showing some benefit, despite how horrible it was at the time.

Max says, "The sun was obscured for a bit, but look, it's over there, so we need to go this direction slightly, and we'll get to the landfill, no problem."

"Exactly," I say, and I head off in that direction with the other three following.

Max's directions were spot on. When we arrive at the landfill, I follow the mole's instructions from his message in the truck's cargo bay. We wind our way amongst piles of trash to one of the processing areas.

We enter what at first feels like a giant room, but the room doesn't have a ceiling. It's not a building. Instead, it's made of blocks of compressed garbage and metal that have been stacked like bricks to form this enclosure. There are several gaps in it, and the stacks don't rise uniformly. We are in what feels like an arena.

A perfect place for an ambush.

A cat awaits us at the far end of the arena. The cat is younger and smaller than I expected. Brown spots accent his dusty black fur. He's a bit mangy, but perhaps that's what a feline freedom fighter looks like.

"Welcome," he says from the far side of the enclosure. "I am Jacques."

"And I am Princess, Empress of the Domain of Rover Boulevard, Slayer of the Wicked Coyote Snarl, and Conqueror over the Megalomaniac, Patches."

"We need to discuss payment," Jacques says, disregarding my credentials. My three companions sit down behind me.

"Our friend on the other side was supposed to pay you. Remember?" I say.

"I've had to change the payment terms," Jacques says. "I have your package, but for you to take it, I will need an extra fifty percent of the catnip payment from you."

"Do you not keep your word? Or, do you fight for freedom without the truth?"

"We are freedom fighters, indeed, and this operation cost much more than expected. We fight for freedom, but not for free."

"Don't you cross me," I say as I squint at Jacques to warn him. I know that the four of us can handle this one young cat without any problem. "We agreed on a price. That's your problem if you can't control your business expenses. If that's what freedom is to you, a business."

"You didn't tell me all the risks of working for you. Freedom is costly."

I emit a low growl, letting Jacques know that I am seriously considering taking the package from him by force.

"Please, Jacques," Fluffy pipes up timidly. I'm about to cut him off, but the usually timid Fluffy has caught me off guard. "We can't pay now, but after this, I promise to spend the rest of my life, if need be, to pay you back. I suffered much under the Emperor while trapped in his domain. His domain is really a large prison. I'm free now, thanks to Princess, but there are still many suffering, and that package is needed to bring my very own brother, Karl, to freedom. He also has been risking his life to defeat the Emperor in the name of freedom. I promise, I will repay you."

Just as I begin to think to myself that Fluffy's speech isn't too bad, a larger cat swoops down on a rope from above, and a dozen ragtag cats pop up around us in the arena. More peek out from the mishmash of garbage that surrounds us.

The larger cat lands gracefully once he releases himself from the rope, and he stands in front of Jacques. An eyepatch conceals one eye, but his other eye gazes deeply into mine. We are now surrounded by cats. Max, Tweedledee, and Fluffy bunch in towards me. My claws extend slowly, but I know I can't win this fight.

The cat wearing the eye patch has light gray fur, and he blinks his one blue eye as he steps towards me. He gives a bow.

"*Bonjour,*" he says. "I am, in truth, *Jacques.*"

"Why...? Who...?"

"I apologize," he continues, "but precautions were necessary to test you. I am pleased to say that, thanks to your companion here, you have passed the test. You may take your package without further payment."

"I don't understand," I say.

"We did the job for this package for money," Jacques says. "I needed to know if you can be trusted, or if you were just another tyrant like the Emperor." Jacques shifts his eyes to Fluffy. "Thankfully for you, Fluffy here revealed your genuine struggle against the Emperor."

"Get the package, you three," I say to my companions. "Head straight to Grand Canyon Drive. We need to put our package to work. I'll catch up."

Once the other three are out of earshot, I say to Jacques, "I need help with one more thing. You will need to pull it off without any interference from Animal Control."

AFTER MY DISCUSSION with Jacques about the next task I have for him, I catch up with the others. We enter my domain and continue to Grand Canyon Drive. Once there, we hide under a bush. As expected, one of the German Shepherds patrols the border. I open the package in front of the other three, and it contains the mini tape recorder I delivered to the mole through Gramma. It also contains four cassette tapes.

"How do we know these will work?" Fluffy asks.

"We need a German Shepherd chasing after one of us," I say. "Otherwise, the German Shepherd might be smart enough to pretend that he's obeying the tape."

"The German Shepherd will chase Fluffy," Tweedledee says. "Those German Shepherds know Fluffy. They have already caught him once, and they must be furious he got away."

"No!" Fluffy says with his eyes wide open.

"I would get caught immediately," Tweedledee says. "I'm not fast enough."

"I will do it," I say to end the argument. "Max is the only one who knows how to operate the tape player. That leaves me as the bait."

"What if it doesn't work?" Fluffy asks. "What will you do to get away from the German Shepherd?"

"It will work," I say.

I have no idea what I would do to get away from the German Shepherd if it doesn't.

Minutes later, we are all in position. The other three hide under a bush facing the Wall. The guard studiously gazes across the Wall in our direction, but he has not spotted us.

The plan is that I will go off to our left a bit, and then I will begin to race across Grand Canyon Drive. Once the guard dog detects me, I will make a sharp right and race down Grand Canyon Drive. Max will start playing the tape. If it works, then the Emperor will have lost control of the German Shepherd, and he will be under our control. If it doesn't work, then I will try to make it up a tree.

Before I head off to the left flank of Max's position, Max realizes something.

"I put the tape labeled, 'Otto,' in the tape player," Max says, "but we don't know if that is Otto. If that German Shepherd is one of the other three, it won't have the voice on the tape."

"Otto typically guards the Wall," Fluffy says

Once I'm in position, I look at Max to make eye contact. He gives me a slight nod, and I see his paw ready to turn the tape player on. I look forward and I sprint out of the bush, directly towards the Wall, Grand Canyon Drive.

My darting is so bold, the German Shepherd freezes as I rush directly at him. He releases a sharp bark and runs at me with his ears folded back. As planned, I turn ninety degrees to my right, and I run along Grand Canyon Dr. As I pass Max, I hear him say, "No volume!" with a mix of fear and frustration.

I can feel the German Shepherd's hot breath on my hind legs after a few more paces, and the barks are closer with each stride.

What is taking so long?! I think to myself.

The German Shepherd will soon have me.

Just as I'm afraid the German Shepherd will pounce on me, a man's voice from the tape player calls out as if over a loudspeaker: "Otto! Go to your pen and stay there and only do what the cats or I tell you to do. Never obey a bird."

As soon as the tape calls out, "Otto!" the German Shepherd halts.

I turn around and watch the German Shepherd trot away with his tail between his legs. Us four cats give a cheer. Fluffy even cries from happiness.

I can't believe it actually worked.

Well, yes, I can. It was my plan, after all.

The mole had recorded the German Shepherds' owners' voices, and he mixed the words on the tapes so that we would have a recording of them commanding the German Shepherds to do what we want. Once we get all of the German Shepherds to listen to the recordings, then the Emperor will be without his henchmen. All who are in the Emperor's domain will be free. This Grand Canyon Drive, the Wall against freedom, is beginning to crumble.

"Sorry, I had forgotten to turn the volume up," Max says.

"It worked out in the end," I say. "Now let's go get those other three German Shepherds."

Max, Tweedledee, Fluffy, and I make our way eagerly towards the Emperor's old house. This is the quickest way to discover the other German Shepherds so that we can cast our spell over them with the tape player.

We encounter the first German Shepherd sooner than I expected. This German Shepherd probably came when it heard Otto's sharp bark when he chased me at the Wall. He is also surprised from seeing us. The sight of four cats boldly strolling around the Emperor's territory must be a shock. His surprise quickly turns to indignation, and he pins his ears to the back of his head as he darts directly at us. But before we can hear his gnashing teeth as he rushes at us, Max plays the tape. I don't hear what the tape says because I am so mesmerized by the effect it has on the German Shepherd. The dog had been previously in full attack mode, but he transforms instantaneously, as if hypnotized, into a totally different creature. He trots away in the opposite direction with his tail between his legs.

This is too easy.

"Two German Shepherds down, and two more to go," I say. "After that, the Emperor will be will be without any of his henchmen."

We continue on towards the Emperor's old house, but we never encounter either of the remaining two German Shepherds. I decide it's best for us to head towards the grocery store and the other shops in the vicinity, but we don't find any German Shepherds over there either.

We rest outside the pizza delivery place as several teenagers sit around inside and pretend to work.

"Can we find my brother and get him out of here now?" Fluffy pleads.

"Not until all four German Shepherds are neutralized," I say. "We have to be certain that all four henchmen are no longer a threat."

"I guess you're right," Fluffy concedes. "Those first two German Shepherds were easy, but I'm worried we will never get Herman. He's sly." We decide to walk around the neighborhood a little bit more. We soon learn why the third German Shepherd was hard to find.

We discover him digging into the burrow of some small animal—perhaps a bunny, groundhog, or even a mole. Dirt flies from between his hind legs as he digs after his terrified prey.

To my delight, the tape player has the same effect on him as it did the other German Shepherds. A delighted mole sticks his head out of the ground and blows kisses at us.

"Thank you, my liberators!" he calls out before diving underground.

"Let's go find that one last German Shepherd," I say to the others as we continue on. "What was his name?"

"His name is Herman," Fluffy says. "And I've got a bad feeling about him."

Before any of us can agree or disagree with Fluffy's sentiments, we hear police sirens screeching around town.

"You never hear police sirens in this town," I say.

"At least not since they had to go help those baby ducklings cross the road," Max says.

My instincts tell me I should go home.

"We've had a good day," I say. "Let's all head home, get some rest, and we'll worry about Herman later." The other three shrug in acquiescence, and we trot towards home.

Not too much later, we arrive at the Wall, Grand Canyon Drive, and we are officially out of the Emperor's new territory. We still have not encountered the last German Shepherd, Herman, and I notice that the sirens have not continued in this direction. They've turned to go somewhere else. At least I know the sirens weren't going to my territory.

But I still have a bad feeling, and so we continue home. It's not that much later when I discover why I had a bad feeling.

The growling and barking of a German Shepherd—it must be Herman—grows louder as I approach my home. Herman is in my domain. He must have special orders from the Emperor himself.

HERMAN TERRORIZES MY DOMAIN.

He has already killed some of my subjects. The skunk who aided me earlier lies limp at the edge of the yard. I don't doubt that Herman targeted the skunk first knowing that the skunk was the only viable weapon against him. There is at least one dead baby rabbit as well. The woodpile that has been stacked up for my whole life against the back fence in my backyard has been knocked over as if he ran up and down it like a treadmill, sending the logs flying.

Herman's most bold statement is his poop and pee under my lilac bush, the very place the Cat Council meets. One baby rabbit apparently wasn't enough, because he's digging for more rabbits, sending grass and dirt flying everywhere.

Where is Animal Control!? Why aren't they doing anything!?

I'm in shock as I take this scene in, but Max acts quickly to get the final cassette tape ready to play. It seems like an eternity, but Max eventually presses the play button, and I hear the click of the tape engaging. What I hear is not what I want to hear. It is a low man's voice, and it starts, "Herrrrrrrmmmmm-maaaaaaaaannnnnnnn."

And then it stops.

The man's voice sounded like slow motion, and it never got past saying the dog's name.

"The batteries died," Max says with a tinge of panic.

"I can get new batteries," Tweedledee says. "Chad got a whole bunch for Christmas."

Tweedledee and Fluffy rush to their house, and I continue to watch Herman destroy my domain. Foaming saliva flies from his mouth as he chews anything in his path. Tweedledee and

Fluffy come back minutes later, but it feels like an eternity has passed.

No people come out of the houses to confront Herman, but I see the big woman person inside on the telephone. Herman is quite the spectacle, and people are afraid of him.

Max puts in new batteries, and he presses the play button again. What comes out is the opposite of what I heard before. It's a high-pitched squiggle sound. And then it stops.

"What was that?" I ask. "The batteries die already?"

"They were brand new!" Tweedledee and Fluffy answer.

Max opens the tape player, and inside we see a giant knot of brown tape that has come out of the cassette.

"It ate the tape!" Max says.

"Can you fix it?"

"It would take hours, even if I had opposable thumbs—and even then it might not work," Max says.

"We don't have time for that," I say. "We need to attack Herman and stop this. He hasn't seen us, so we have the advantage of surprise."

"Are you crazy?" Fluffy says. "That's Herman, not just some dog."

"I have defeated the worst of the coyotes," I say. "And there are four of us, and I say we can take out Herman."

In reality, I'm not so certain. I'm relieved to look at Max and see him nodding in agreement.

"I will get Herman to chase me under that chain-link fence," I say. "The rest of you need to attack him while he's going under the fence. This is the trick I used to defeat that horrible coyote, Captain One-Eyed Jack. It is the best chance we have against Herman."

I race towards Herman to swipe at his tail, but he detects

me. He turns and locks his dark eyes on me. I veer to the side and race towards the chain-link fence. Herman follows, and I pass under the fence.

Herman doesn't follow. Instead, he leaps over the chain-link fence and bowls over the other three cats. With two quick swipes of his paws, he sends Tweedledee and then Fluffy flying. They thwack against the fence and fall to the ground, unconscious.

Herman focuses all his attention on Max. Max gets in a few good strikes, but Herman launches him against the fence.

Herman barrels towards me, baring his teeth. I back up and dash from side to side, swiping tentatively. Herman is merely toying with me.

I give one sharp *yeowl*, try to leap onto his back, but I miss. I attempt to disengage, but not before Herman catches me in his jaws, shakes me, and then tosses me.

Herman backs me into a corner, and I know that I have no chance against him.

"Meow!" Max cries out, releasing his signature pathetic meow for help. For once, I don't mind it!

Why isn't Animal Control doing anything? Where are they?

Herman is clearly causing damage and injury!

I have no choice but to fight Herman. I must engage in a fight that I know I have no chance of winning.

Herman comes in for the kill. He sees that I'm already injured.

I resolve to fight with dignity against this beast, but then I hear a deep and bold voice that is unlike any voice I've heard.

"Halt!"

I look over and I see that Chief has let himself out of his pen.

He has never yelled with such authority.

"Pick on somebody your own size!" Chief demands.

Herman is caught off guard for a second, confused by the sight of this overweight and elderly dog challenging him.

Chief rushes upon a startled Herman, attempting to smother him with his girth and clamp down with his giant jaws. Chief squashes Herman with his weight and sinks his teeth in, but his teeth and jaws are old. Herman breaks away and does the same to Chief. I admire Chief for putting up a noble fight, but it's clear that Herman, the younger and stronger fighter, will emerge victorious.

I try to join the fight to help Chief, but my broken body won't allow it.

Then I see something.

Herman convulses, his body slightly contracting, but then he continues fighting.

What are these convulsions?

After a few more slight convulsions, Herman lets out a squeal, releases Chief, and looks about frantically. One of his eyes is bloodied. Chief tries to attack again as Herman pulls away, but he's too weak to clamp on with his jaws.

Herman lets out a few more shrieks of pain, and his one good eye looks past me, and it's full of fear.

What is happening to Herman?

I turn my head to see what Herman is looking at, and I see the middle boy child pumping his BB gun, aiming, and then silently firing again. Herman whimpers, and then he limps away. The middle boy child continues to fire BBs into him with his BB gun. Herman escapes from the yard and staggers down the road towards the Wall, but he collapses in the middle of Rover Boulevard.

10

I go in and out of consciousness. I don't know if I'm like this for minutes, hours, or days. I only vaguely sense that my people gently pick me up and put me in a car.

I am willingly going to the veterinarian.

I remember the cold steel table, the bright lights, but when I wake up, my body is stiff and achy.

Laying in my favorite sunbeam, I must be dreaming.

Have I died and gone to heaven?

I look over, and Max lies nearby, bandaged up. Obviously, I'm not in heaven. I try to stretch and move, but I can't move fluidly.

"She's awake," the oldest girl child says excitedly. She comes over with the other children, and they are eager to feed me encouragement.

If the middle boy child had not saved my life by shooting Herman repeatedly with his BB gun, I would not be tolerating all of their attention right now. It seems that Max has been awake for a while because they are not paying much attention to him. The children not only give me encouragement, but they also give me news.

"You'll be just fine in a day or so," the oldest girl child says. "It hurts now, but you'll be walking around fine tomorrow. It looks worse than it really is."

In a day or so? How long has it been? I can't miss my New Year's Eve meeting with the Emperor at the old gas station!

"If Chief hadn't gotten into the fight," the middle boy child says, "then it would have been much worse."

The children continue talking, but the doorbell rings, and I strain my ears to hear who is at the door.

"Yes?" the big man person says. He strongly dislikes it when strangers ring the doorbell and come to talk.

"I'm from Animal Control," a man says.

"You're a little late," the big man person says, raising his voice.

"I'm here to apologize and explain," the Animal Control man responds. "We were transporting a dangerous dog who had to be put to sleep to another facility. Our vehicle got into an accident. We crashed. We are okay now, but we couldn't respond to any calls. It's only now that we got the vehicle repaired and we've been released from the hospital. We've heard all these messages about an emergency involving some crazy German Shepherd."

"I don't see you guys my whole life," the big man person says, "but the one time that I do need you, you're unavailable because you've gotten into a car accident. What are the odds of that?"

"Like I said," the Animal Control man says, "I'm just here to apologize."

"Well, apology accepted. That's just the way the cookie crumbles sometimes."

I now know what the Emperor was doing when he was absent the other night when we tried to attack him. He was out hatching an evil scheme, which included doing something that would crash the Animal Control vehicle so that it could not respond to Herman attacking my territory.

Were we able to foil his plot by shooting Herman with the BB gun, or is there more to his plan? It's too much for me to ponder right now, and so I lay my head down to rest.

Later that day, my people send me outside so that I can go to the bathroom. Tweedledee and Fluffy come to visit. They were knocked out of the fight early on, but they were not hurt badly. The first thing I say to the other cats in the Cat Council is, "Once I'm better tomorrow, we're going to go over and get Fluffy's brother, Karl."

"What about that New Year's Eve meeting in just three days with the Emperor at the old gas station?" Max asks.

"Without the German Shepherds," I respond, "we have all the power. We are in control now. I'll demand that the Emperor releases his new territory. I can probably take it for myself. In addition to that, he will have to give us oversight in his older territory. Without his German Shepherds, he doesn't have any power."

"I'm going to go with Tweedledee and get my brother, Karl, right now and bring him home," Fluffy says, obviously uninterested in what I had to say about the upcoming New Year's Eve meeting with the Emperor. I've forgotten that this has been Fluffy's main concern all along: his brother. Usually timid, I see a defiance in Fluffy that I've never seen before, and I want to reward it.

"Very well," I say. "You and Tweedledee can go get your brother and being bring him back over here."

Max and I have to go back inside and continue our recovery, but our people put us in the garage at night. Tweedledee and Fluffy return from the Emperor's territory and come to talk to us in the garage. The defiant look has left Fluffy, and fear has crept back into his eyes.

Something is wrong.

I sense it as soon as they come into the garage.

"We searched everywhere," Fluffy says, "but we can't find my brother, Karl. The Emperor has done something with him." Tweedledee tries to comfort Fluffy as best she can, but I think Fluffy is right.

Maybe we don't have all the power for the negotiation on New Year's Eve with the Emperor.

THE NEXT DAY, I go to Chief's pen to talk to him. He's not there.

Maybe Chief didn't pull through.

But if that were the case, certainly the others would've told me.

Then I see Chief inside his owner's house. Like usual, he's laying and resting, but I can see his owners poking and prodding him to gauge his health. Chief sleeps a lot, but he'll respond when he's poked and prodded like that.

I can't hear what his owners are saying, but I sense that it's not good. His man owner is shrugging his shoulders and holding his palms out as he is saying something to the woman. I think he is saying, "I don't know, I don't know," while she shakes her head slightly. I've got a bad feeling that Chief's final battle with Herman has convinced his owners that he's gotten too old, and they need to send him away, never to be brought back again. They will put Chief to sleep.

I knead my claws in anger as I consider the fact that the Emperor, who is ultimately responsible for Chief's injuries, still temporarily lives under the same roof while his owners are away on vacation.

We have another emergency Cat Council meeting that day. Even Tweedledee accepts that it is essential, given the circumstances.

"Max, Fluffy, and I will meet the Emperor on New Year's Eve at the old gas station," I announce to the others. "There, we will put our demands to the Emperor. The Emperor will give up his new territory and leave my territory alone. He will be able to keep his old territory, as long as it is inspected regularly by Jacques to ensure that he has not found a way to oppress others. Once the Emperor is stripped of his power, we should be able to find Karl."

"But what if the old gas station is a trap?" Fluffy asks.

"I've been there," I assure him. "It's empty. Condemned by the E.P.A.: the Environmental Protection Agency. Without German Shepherds, the Emperor has no force to back up his demands. Besides, I have another plan of action to make sure the Emperor moves out of my territory for good. Tweedledee has a mission with Jacques that is just as vital as our mission at the old gas station. It's better that the rest of you don't know all the details."

"I'll go with Fluffy early," Max offers, "to make sure the gas station is unchanged. We need to see if it is still empty, and if the Emperor has put in any traps. You need to stay here and heal up until New Year's Eve."

I can't disagree with that, but my fur bristles at the idea of showing weakness.

"It's not so much that I need rest," I say, "but I do have other important plans to work on."

"THE GAS STATION WAS EMPTY, as expected," Max reports the next day. "But there was something else abnormal."

"Animals were leaving the Emperor's territory as quickly as they could," Fluffy says. "Most of them were merely following the crowd, and nobody we asked could give a real reason why they were leaving. They were frightened, though."

"There was something dangerous," Max adds.

"A few of the fleeing animals mentioned something," Fluffy says.

"What, exactly?" I ask.

Max and Fluffy look at each other, afraid to admit something.

"It seems funny now that I'm about to say it out loud," Max says, "but we heard about some kind of monster."

"But you didn't encounter anything that was a monster, did you?" I say.

Max and Fluffy look at each other, and they don't have to answer, "No."

"The Emperor is a master at such things, like all tyrants," I say. "Through fear, he makes everybody believe he is in control, even when he really is not, and especially when you can't see how he exerts his control. The reality is that, without his German Shepherds, he's lost his power, and so he has to use tricks and manipulation—like a monster. The most powerful fear can come when its source is ambiguous."

"But my brother is still missing," Fluffy adds.

Tweedledee interrupts us, having returned from her mission.

"Jacques says everything is in place," Tweedledee reports. "But he did say he lost a cat. He's not sure why."

"I'm sure that happens from time to time in his line of work," I say.

"It could be the monster," Fluffy says as his eyes widen.

"They recovered the body," Tweedledee says. "He wasn't eaten by a coyote or hit by a car. He was killed for sport."

This last bit gives me a chill.

With Max and Fluffy's report, I was convinced the Emperor was desperate and using tricks to control others through fear. But this death can hardly be a coincidence. The Emperor must have a secret, and I'm afraid it will show itself at the old gas station on New Year's Eve.

11

December 31, New Year's Eve day, finally arrives. The Emperor's owners are still on vacation, and so the Emperor continues to live at Chief's house.

As best as I can tell, the Emperor is only in the house when Chief's owner goes to check on him at lunchtime. He has been sneaking in and out of the house somehow, but I can't figure out how. I only see him fly away and return. He is a cunning bird. It makes no difference to me, though. I'm looking forward to his surrender tonight at the old gas station.

I'm about to go make final preparations for tonight, but then a car pulls into our new neighbor's driveway. Three older boys get out. Clad in winter coats, they smile and laugh. They give each other high-fives as they wheel coolers to their parents' new house. These must be the neighbors' college-age kids. But why would they come back while their parents are away?

Later that afternoon, loud music rumbles within their house as colored lights spin around inside. Those college kids are going to have a New Year's Eve party at their house tonight while their parents are gone.

Interesting. That may help my plan.

Time drags through the day, but eventually the four of us cats march towards the old gas station. I smile proudly as we cross Grand Canyon Drive, which, until recently, had been an impenetrable Wall guarded by German Shepherds. Once across, I send Tweedledee away on her own mission.

"We'll be back home tonight before you know it," I say.

"I hope so," Tweedledee says. "This is all too much for me. I'm not meant to be going on missions. What do I do if you don't come back?"

"You will need to grow up fast. You will be the only cat, and you will be in charge." I add, "We will be back. Focus on your mission."

Tweedledee departs on her own, but after a few seconds, she pauses and turns back towards us. "I don't feel safe somehow..."

"Go!" I say to urge her on. I press on with Max, but Fluffy hesitates to follow until Tweedledee is out of sight.

On the way to the gas station, we pass several houses whose occupants have the same idea as our new neighbors' college-age kids. Loud music and flashing lights parties inside.

When we pass the pizza delivery business, several cars zoom away and return to deliver pizzas. It will not close down, even for this holiday. When we arrive at the old gas station, however, it's silent.

Just as Max and Fluffy reported, it appears unchanged from when I saw it previously. The yellow tape with the writing, "CONDEMNED BY E.P.A.," still warns people away.

I'm finally going to topple the regime of that Emperor parrot.

"I will do all the talking," I remind Max and Fluffy. "You two only help me if we need to use force. There is no way a silly parrot can handle three cats."

We walk past the yellow E.P.A. warning tape and enter the old gas station through the broken front door.

According to plan, Max and Fluffy spread out on either side of me. The gas station is well lit by the moonlight that streams in through the large gaps in the roof and ceiling. I see more sky than ceiling.

Before I spot the Emperor, he calls out to me.

"You have come to comply with my conditions?"

"I have come so that you may comply with my conditions," I counter.

The Emperor releases a loud, cackling laugh that I remember from a movie my people had seen about a girl who goes to a land called Oz.

"We've defeated your mighty German Shepherds," I say, looking about to find the parrot. "There are three of us who can force you to comply, if need be. You will forfeit your new territories, but you may keep your old territories with regular inspections by a party of my choosing."

"Ha!" the Emperor responds.

"You and your owners will be moving out of my territory soon, whether you like it or not."

I can't wait until that part of my plan comes to fruition.

"But I have something," the Emperor says, "or somebody, that you want."

One of the doors in the gas station opens. The open door reveals the mole, Fluffy's brother, Karl. He shivers. His fur is matted down, and his ridiculous Christmas sweater is dirty and torn.

"Brother!" Fluffy gasps.

"What will you bargain for this traitor?" the Emperor says.

"I will let you live," I say. I, of course, knew that the Emperor had probably captured the mole and would use him as a bargaining chip. "In return for your life, you give us Fluffy's brother. Your German Shepherds can't save you now. I know you crashed the Animal Control truck so that Animal Control would be unable to catch Herman at my house. But even that didn't stop me."

"Oh," the Emperor says, "I forgot to mention one thing, didn't I? How could I forget this one thing?"

I'm sure the Emperor is bluffing, but then he somehow opens a door next to the mole.

The open door reveals a stocky dog the size of a German Shepherd. He has short, reddish-brown fur with black splotches. His fierce appearance matches his ugliness. His one brown eye is fixated on me, and his other red eye doesn't look quite straight. As he snaps his jaws, I see a gap where one of his fangs should be. His ears are trimmed, and so is his tail. This dog is not meant for shepherding sheep; this dog is meant for fighting.

"Sit!" Emperor calls out. The dog gnashes his teeth, but he obeys the Emperor and sits. Both Max and Fluffy sit as well.

"This is my Super Soldier. He has never had a person as an owner, and so he only obeys my voice. Animal Control had captured him and they were on their way to put him to sleep. I feared that I would lose my precious Super Soldier. But then I was able to crash the Animal Control truck and rescue my Super Soldier. I saved my Super Soldier from death row!"

"Herman was really sent to prevent me from meddling in your plans with the Animal Control truck," I say as I realize the truth, "and not so that Animal Control couldn't stop Herman."

I also realize that this Super Soldier must be the dog Animal Control captured on Thanksgiving night, the night *Mozart* went missing. It seems so long ago now. Max also sensed this beast when he was in Animal Control.

"Exactly," the Emperor says. "Now, Super Soldier, attack them!"

It's the last thing I hear before the Super Soldier barrels towards me.

I READY myself to dodge as the Super Soldier dog pounces, but a blinding white light illuminates the inside of the old gas station like a bolt of lightning.

The bright light startles everybody, and it allows me to evade the Super Soldier. I look to the sky through the gaping holes in the roof, and I see fireworks exploding in the sky to celebrate the arrival of the new year. A fraction of a second later, the loud booms from the fireworks rattle my bones.

Us cats climb to the top of a high shelf, out of the Super Soldier's reach. The Emperor flies about the rafters of the decaying gas station, squawking to taunt us.

The Super Soldier leaps at us as we huddle together on top of the empty store shelf. The mole huddles in the doorway in fear. The Super Soldier is perfectly obedient to the Emperor; he attacks us, but ignores the mole. The Super Soldier's jaws snap just millimeters below us, and we barely fit on top of the shelf.

The Emperor circles about us in the air, and he sends forth his mockery.

"You can't hide forever," he calls out. "You will soon fall into the jaws of my Super Soldier."

Thud!

The shelving unit rattles, and I look down. The Super Soldier has taken a running start and rammed the shelf with his head. If he can't leap up to reach us at the top of the shelf, then he is committed to knocking this metal shelf over.

Thud! Thud!

The shelf system is holding, but I know it won't last long. It rocks more with each thud from the battering ram that is the Super Soldier's head. Max, Fluffy, and I slip around on the metallic top, barely able to stay on.

The Emperor continues to fly about, hurling insults, and I can see his silhouette against the New Year's Eve fireworks, but then his silhouette takes a sudden change of direction.

My eyes dart about to find where the Emperor went. He lies on one of the horizontal ceiling beams recovering from an attack. He sees something, and he flies directly towards... *Moonbeam.*

Moonbeam is a predator and much faster than the Emperor, but the Emperor has a larger and stronger beak, and talons to match.

Moonbeam silently darts around the interior of the gas station with amazing agility. The Emperor thrashes about, sending his feathers flying. It is a battle between the larger and slower Emperor and the smaller and faster Moonbeam.

The Super Soldier continues smashing into our shelf. It teeters, perilously close to falling over. Moonbeam is going to have to defeat the Emperor soon if we are to escape from his Super Soldier.

Two other owls join the fight. They must be Moonbeam's family members whom he brought to my territory. The three owls swirl and swoop around the Emperor, confusing him. Seconds later, the owls grab onto the Emperor with their talons and drive him into the ground.

The three owls pin the Emperor to the ground, and Moonbeam yells at the Emperor, "Command your Super Soldier to stop!"

"Never!" the Emperor rasps. Moonbeam digs his talons in deeper to force the Emperor to call off his Super Soldier.

"*ARRRGGGHHHHHH!* Okay, I promise to call him off," the Emperor says in desperation. The three owls loosen their grip, and the Emperor composes himself before he calls out, "Super Soldier!"

The Super Soldier turns his head to the Emperor and pauses his assault on the shelf.

"Super Soldier, you must—"

But before the Emperor can give the command, Karl, the mole, comes seemingly out of nowhere and pounces on top of the Emperor parrot, pushing the owls aside.

Karl snaps his jaws to permanently silence the Emperor.

"Brother! No!" Fluffy yells.

Fluffy tumbles off the shelf from astonishment.

The Super Soldier snatches Fluffy out of the air, shakes him, and then hurls his body against the wall.

Fluffy lies still on the ground.

The owls fly up into the rafters as the Super Soldier rushes to his injured master. Karl rushes towards the exit. The Super

Soldier whimpers questioningly to discover if his master is alive.

"I am the true Emperor," Karl announces triumphantly in front of the exit, "and that parrot was my servant, until he became too powerful for his own good."

The Super Soldier releases a mournful howl announcing the parrot's death, and I say to the others, "Let's get out of here! Moonbeam, fly Fluffy home."

The Super Soldier growls and advances towards Karl, the one responsible for his master's death. Before he gets too close, Karl pulls a tiny spray can out from under his sweater and sprays it at the Super Soldier. A noxious cloud—it must be some kind of pepper spray—temporarily blinds the Super Soldier and makes him yelp in pain.

I knew it. His goofy cat sweater had a purpose beyond poor fashion sense!

Karl rushes out to escape. I consider pursuing him, but I must get away from the Super Soldier.

Max and I leap to the ground as Moonbeam swoops down to grab Fluffy. We rush out of the old gas station towards my house. We don't pause to look back, even when we hear the Super Soldier's howls turn to distant barks. We don't stop until we arrive at home.

Red and blue lights from a police car illuminate our new neighbor's front yard. The fireworks have stopped, and the lights inside the new neighbor's house are on, but they're not spinning. The music is off. Chad's parents next door frantically care for Fluffy who has—mysteriously to them—shown up injured on their doorstep.

I'M TORN between watching the police break up the New Year's Eve party and talking with the cats about what happened.

Max starts to say something, but I shush him when I see the policemen inspecting the driveway and the ground near the garage with their flashlights. One police officer passes around the whole house, carefully inspecting the ground illuminated by his flashlight. When he's done, he speaks with one of the other officers. In turn, he speaks urgently into his radio.

This part of my plan is going perfectly.

"What in the world happened back there?" Max asks.

"That loudmouth parrot never was the Emperor," I say. "The mole, Karl, Fluffy's brother, was the real Emperor all along." I myself have a hard time believing it as we continue to watch the policeman spoil the New Year's Eve party.

"So that's why the mole ended the parrot's life before he could call off his Super Soldier," Max says. "The parrot was the only one who could command the Super Soldier, and the mole, or the true Emperor, I guess, didn't want the Super Soldier to stop attacking us."

"And his own brother, Fluffy, lost his life because of it."

"Do you think Fluffy was really on the Emperor's side too?" Max asks. "Or did Karl have his own brother fooled?"

"My instincts tell me that Fluffy really was on our side, but we may never know," I say.

"Those owls showed up at just the right time," Max says. "Lucky us."

I give Max a look as if to say, "Come on. That was not luck."

"What? How? Don't tell me..." Max says

"I've got friends in high places, I guess," I say. Max shakes his head and doesn't bother to ask more. He's learned that when I'm cryptic, I'm not going to reveal my secrets. I watch with amusement as the police kick partygoers out of the new neighbors' house.

"Did you have any idea about Karl the mole being the real Emperor?" Max says. "I had no idea."

"The only thing I can think of," I say, "is that Herman pooped under the lilac bush, exactly where the Cat Council meets. It could have been a coincidence, but Karl the mole was the only outsider who knew where the Cat Council meets."

"I never thought of that," Max says. "But why would Karl the mole go through all that trouble of using a parrot and pretending to be a spy?"

"He bet I would find a way to defeat the parrot and the Super Soldier," I say. "Then, having infiltrated my domain, he could have also infiltrated Jacques' group of freedom fighters. At just the right time, he would betray us both, and take over in one fell swoop. The parrot had grown too powerful, and he feared the parrot would use the Super Soldier against him. When the Super Soldier was on the verge of eating us, Karl had no choice but to end the parrot. Extremely cunning, if you think about it. I'm flattered he thought I could defeat the parrot and his Super Soldier."

"Yeah, but," Max started, "you weren't able to defeat the parrot and his Super Soldier."

"My plan hasn't yet completely unfolded," I say with a nod towards the police inspecting the neighbor's yard.

"Another thing," Max says, "is that we thought the parrot was the Emperor because of how old the Emperor was. The parrot blinded Gramma, who is really old."

"I suspect 'The Emperor' is simply a title," I explain, "passed from the master tyrant to his apprentice. The parrot served the previous cat who held the title of Emperor. In truth, 'The Emperor' is far more ancient than even that parrot."

"Look over there," Max says. "Here comes Tweedledee, back from her mission with Jacques."

I'm glad to see Tweedledee briskly trotting towards us. Before she says anything, I know by her gait that her mission was a success.

"Jacques had already completed part one of the plan," Tweedledee reports, "and part two will be on January 2, the day after tomorrow. The garbage trucks don't run until then."

"Perfect," I say. "I just hope that Chief makes it until then."

"Say," Tweedledee asks, "where's Fluffy?"

What I have to say next to Tweedledee is one of the most challenging things of being a leader of a domain. I go on to explain to Tweedledee how, in addition to her brother leaving her, she may have now lost her newest friend, Fluffy.

As exhausted as I am the next day, New Year's Day, I have a hard time sleeping. I'm looking for something to happen. I don't know exactly what I'm looking for, but I will know it when I see it. Now that the parrot is dead, this part of my plan is not essential, but I didn't know the parrot would be gone at this point. As an empress, few things are more fulfilling than watching your plans unfold just as you had hoped, and that is exactly what happens on this morning. Mostly.

At about 9 AM, a van pulls up to our new neighbor's house. On the side of the van are three large letters: "E.P.A."

The Environmental Protection Agency. Just the people I was hoping for.

A few men get out of the van, examine the driveway and ground encircling the new neighbor's house, and then they put on some goofy looking white plastic suits. Then, they collect dirt samples from around the house. I wish I could tell them that what they found is car battery acid and anti-freeze, recently dumped by Jacques, but they must discover that for themselves. It is quite the environmental hazard to have such toxic chemicals dumped onto the ground. The E.P.A. should condemn this house, just as they condemned the old gas station. But that is not the whole of my plan. The most crucial part of my plan unfolds when the men are about to get in their van to leave.

"*Who?*" rings out from the top of the evergreen tree in the new neighbor's backyard.

The E.P.A. men take no notice.

Moonbeam calls out again: "*Who?*"

"Is that an owl I hear—and during the day?" one of the EPA men says. They all look up into the tree. Since the evergreen is the solitary tree in the new neighbor's backyard, they soon spot Moonbeam sitting on his branch.

"Is that what I think it is?" one man asks another.

Bingo, I think to myself.

The Environmental Protection Agency has just discovered an endangered species living in a yard with illegally dumped toxic waste.

Perfect.

"ALL WE CAN DO IS WAIT," Max says as he looks around for bugs to play with outside. He can't find any this time of year.

"Let's see how Chief is doing," I say as I head towards Chief's pen. Max follows, and we hop up onto the fence. Chief is still lying inside his owner's house, unresponsive.

"I just hope this tells Chief's owner that Chief has friends and he shouldn't put Chief to sleep."

"Yeah," Max says.

Snow isn't falling, but I can see my breath on this cold New Year's Day, even in the afternoon. Everything is silent, until I hear muffled crying. It's more like sniffling.

Max and I walk along the fence to see what it is. We discover Chad huddled up in his backyard, and he's crying. It's no doubt because Tweedledum left, and now Fluffy is gone. Chad must be crying because his parents were unable to save Fluffy's life. For the first time in my life, I feel sorry for somebody other than my own people.

I look up, and I see Tweedledee coming towards us on the fence.

The three of us sit and listen to Chad cry.

"Go comfort Chad," I tell Tweedledee. "Rub against him and purr."

"You, of all cats," Tweedledee says, "are giving me this advice?"

"People can be incredibly emotional," I explain. "Especially about pets, and sometimes they just need a little extra help."

Tweedledee shrugs, hops down from the fence and goes to rub against Chad and purr. Max and I head back to Chief's pen to keep watch. We are rewarded not too much later when Chief's owner opens his backdoor, leaves it open, and then disappears for a few seconds. Shortly after, he's red-faced and struggling to carry Chief out the door to his pen. I sit up perfectly straight, and my ears twitch around to take in every possible detail. Chief's owner huffs and puffs, and he eventually places Chief, quite a large dog, in his pen.

Chief's owner says, "I guess you should spend your last day

in your favorite spot with your friends." After a few more deep breaths, the owner drags Chief to the entrance of his doghouse. Chief is dead weight.

His owner said that this is Chief's last day. I only have until tomorrow. The vet must not be open today, but tomorrow the vet will be open. And the vet will put Chief to sleep. Chief's owner goes inside with his head hanging low.

"I guess you haven't heard, have you, Chief?" I say to Chief. Chief gives no sign of hearing my voice. Max and I tell the whole story about how that cunning cat who was the mole, Karl, was the real Emperor, but he ended up losing his brother, Fluffy, for it. At one point, I pause my story and I lean in excitedly because Chief has lifted his eyebrows slightly, but then I decide I can't know if it's because of something I said, or if it's just a nervous twitch.

At the end of the story, I say, "So here we are now, and we just want to see you walk and talk—be your usual old Chief self. We don't want to lose you, and you only have until tomorrow to get better."

"I think we need to say thank you to Chief," Max says. I feel like I just thanked Chief for making a mess in Chad's yard. But for once, Max has said something wise. It is something Chief himself would say.

"Thanks, Chief," I say. "Thanks for giving me advice and being a trusted and loyal adviser, even when I'm brash and arrogant." I look over to Max, and he's clearly expecting me to say more.

"And thanks for facing Herman," I say. "It wasn't in vain. It wasn't in vain." I stop because I'm not sure I can continue talking to Chief without crying, and I don't want to cry in front of Max. I look over and see tears dripping down Max's face. I'm afraid I'll be next, but I'm saved by the slamming of a large van door.

I rush over to the new neighbor's house, and Max follows behind me. The large van door slamming was from an E.P.A. vehicle. If I didn't know that Chief's end was imminent, I would be chuckling as I watch the E.P.A. men. They hang a border of yellow tape around the house. Then they put up signs declaring the house condemned. No people are allowed to live there.

Another E.P.A. man comes out of the van with a very large camera, and he zooms in on Moonbeam. I hear the camera click multiple times as he takes photographs of Moonbeam and his family.

Chad's mom comes out of their house to talk to the E.P.A. men who are condemning their neighbor's house.

"This land will hereby be protected by the Environmental Protection Agency," one of the men says to Chad's mom. "The owners of this house illegally dumped hazardous material, but they also did it in an ecosystem supporting an endangered owl." The man points up to the top of the large evergreen tree in the backyard. "A rare owl and his family live up there. The people who live here will have to move out, and the E.P.A. will have to make sure that this ecosystem is completely stable so that those owls can flourish."

I listen as they continue talking. I smile because the E.P.A. will not allow coyotes or anything else to disturb my ecosystem, my domain. I got the brilliant idea from my first visit to the old gas station, also condemned by the E.P.A.

That night, I lay by Chief in his doghouse and hope that it's not the last time I see him. I do cry this night, and I hope that Chief cares, and that he just can't respond because his health is so bad. I sleep fitfully through the tears, but I come wide-awake when I hear a howling dog from far off. That Super Soldier is still on the loose. I hope Animal Control gets him soon. I'm so exhausted from my previous adventures, though, I fall into a deep sleep.

The loud metallic squeals of a garbage truck wake me up early the next morning, on the second of January. I rub against Chief, but he doesn't respond. He's nearly comatose.

I rush over to the garbage truck, and I'm thrilled to see Jacques emerge with somebody else. Tweedledee comes running and calls out, "Gramma! Gramma!" as Jacques leads Gramma off the garbage truck.

"Don't squeeze me too tight, Dee," Gramma says as Tweedledee embraces her. "My joints are achy. It's sure gonna snow."

GRAMMA WAS RIGHT. Snow starts to fall, slowly at first as we lead Gramma to Chief's pen. By the time we arrive, the snow is coming down hard. I can feel the heavy flakes dropping onto my coat and melting almost immediately, but after a few minutes, they don't melt fast enough, and snow builds up on me.

"I hear an old dog breathing nearby," Gramma says. "What's he doing? Is he about dead or something?"

"He's not dead, but he's going to be," I say.

"He just needs a good friend, Gramma," Tweedledee says. "You are still so full of life. Chief will have a reason to stick around if you just talk about old stories with him."

"I don't know about that," Gramma says.

"At least try to help him get better," I say. "He's going to go to the vet for the last time later today, if you know what I mean.

But if he shows some signs of life, I don't think his owners will take him."

"Gramma will see what she can do."

Tweedledee leads Gramma down into Chief's pen. Gramma tries to enter the doghouse to get out of the snow, but Chief blocks the way.

"I thought an old dog like you would have some manners. You must've forgotten them in your old age." The doghouse's overhang partially shields Gramma.

"Look! Squirrel!" Grandma calls out.

Chief remains as still as a possum playing dead.

"It was worth a try..."

Gramma tries another tactic.

"You see that show with a nice old lady who solves mysteries? You wouldn't believe what was in the last episode."

Chief shows no signs of hearing Gramma. She recounts the whole episode, but Chief is still content to let the snow accumulate on him quietly.

Grandma changes her tactic again.

"I bet I could beat you in bridge or pinochle with my eyes closed," Gramma says. "Not that I can see a blessed thing anyways these days!" She lets out a laugh at her own joke, but Chief doesn't take up the challenge for bridge or pinochle.

I look over at Max and Tweedledee, and they look back with concern. Gramma is not working.

"At least you will live near Gramma now," I tell Tweedledee.

Gramma continues on with Chief.

"Your father wouldn't have given up like this," Gramma says. "I heard you risked your life, fighting off a German Shepherd. There was obviously something worth fighting for. Why not stick around and enjoy it?"

I don't believe what I see at first, and so I don't say anything. But I think I see the snow fall off as Chief raises one of his eyebrows.

"My father?" Chief says.

I do believe it now.

Chief shakes snow off his head, and he looks at Gramma. Before Gramma can answer, though, we all yell out, "Chief!"

We all tumble down into Chief's pen, rush over to him, and give him hugs.

"We thought we were going to lose you," I say. Everybody nods in agreement.

"I don't remember anything," Chief says. "I only remember staring down that mean German Shepherd, Herman. After that, I don't know. Out of the fog, I just heard somebody mention my father. I never knew him. I want to know about my father before I have to leave this world."

"You are just like your father," Gramma says. "Your father tried to save me when the Emperor and his dogs were attacking me, years ago. Just like you stepped in to save Princess. You succeeded. Unfortunately, your father failed."

I can't believe that Chief's father is the dog who tried to save Gramma from that parrot, years ago!

We are excited that Chief is going to live, confident that his owners won't take him to the vet now that he is awake from his coma.

Grandma goes on to tell Chief more about his father, and later that afternoon, there's another snowball fight between the neighborhood kids. Chief and Gramma take it all in from his pen like spectators.

Chief's owner and his wife can't believe their dog's recovery.

"I don't know how, but it looks like Chief's getting better," his owner says. "And we somehow got a new cat out of it."

"We have to keep her," his wife says. "I think she saved Chief's life. Looks like Chief and that old cat are fixing to be best of friends."

I remember what Gramma said the first time I met her: "Our history is what makes us who we are today and gives our lives meaning. We can't afford to forget our past, or we die— figuratively, and literally."

Chief was brought back to life by discovering his own history.

A few days later, the heavy snow has melted. The kids go back to school this morning. The holidays are finally over, and my domain and I survived. Not a bad holiday season, really, all things considered.

I survived a maniacal spy plot involving brainwashed German Shepherds and a tyrannical parrot. I'm sad for Fluffy, even though I never really knew him that well. But I'm thankful for Gramma and Chief. I do wonder if that Super Soldier ever successfully hunted down Karl for destroying his master, the parrot. I no longer hear the Super Soldier's howls at night. Animal Control must have captured him again. It tires me just to think about it, so I lay down to sleep. Now that the holidays are over, I can get some rest, confident Moonbeam will watch over my domain while I sleep.

THE END.

Author's Notes:

I have always wanted to write a Cold War spy novel, and this is it. Writing a true spy novel is insanely difficult. Accurately recreating settings and timelines from places I've never been and from before I lived is massively time consuming. Instead, I placed such a spy novel within Princess' world.

The reader probably noticed that Princess' town was like Berlin during the Cold War. One part was her domain, and Grand Canyon Drive served as the Wall that divided it in half. The fierce German Shepherds served as stand ins for both the feared East German secret police, the Stasi, and the border guards who had to keep people inside of East Berlin. Obviously, the Wall in Berlin was, generally, east of those who lived in West Berlin. In Princess' town, Grand Canyon Drive was in fact more generally West from where she lived on Rover Boulevard. I figured it was worth it to fudge on the direction for the sake of matching Berlin. I considered changing the name of Grand Canyon Drive to Mauer Drive, which means "Wall" in German, but I wanted Princess' fans to be able to visit Grand Canyon Drive itself.

Just as *Princess the Cat Saves the Farm* paid homage to several children's chapter books, this book pays homage to many Cold War spy novels.

Many Cold War spy novels have what I call a "Wall Scene," or, a "Wall Watching Scene." That is, the hero impatiently waits for a spy, source, or agent, to cross the Berlin Wall into West Berlin, where they would find freedom. Of course, the escaping spy sometimes never shows up, and the hero wonders if the secret police captured the spy. Or, the hero may watch as the spy is arrested at the border, or even gunned down in no-man's land, having seemingly been granted passage to West Berlin, only to be stopped before they officially reach West Berlin. These scenes serve as a motivator for the hero, or they set out the challenge for the hero. In Princess' case, her agent, code-named *Mozart*, never showed up at the Wall. For Princess, this aroused suspicion that something was going wrong.

Mozart was a carefully chosen code name. Mozart is perhaps the most well known classical composer, but it was also chosen as an homage to Len Deighton's famous Cold War spy novel, *Berlin Game* (the first in a nine part series). In it, the spy network all had names of classical composers, and at the beginning, if I remember correctly, *Brahms* had gone missing.

The reader will also note that communist police states like East Germany were oppressive, but so are radical states that are right leaning, such as the fascism that ruled in Germany before the Cold War. The political viewpoints may be radically different, but the oppression often looks the same. In recognition of this, the monstrous dog who served as the Emperor's secret weapon and enforcer was given the title, "Super Soldier." Its initials are "SS," from Hitler's terrifying enforcers during World War II.

The last homage is that of the identity of the true Emperor. Fluffy's brother, Karl, had been the real Emperor all along. John LeCarre's famous Karla Trilogy, beginning with *Tinker, Tailor, Soldier, Spy*, focuses on the Soviet super spy, Karla. Karla wouldn't serve as a good name for a cat, but Karl conceivably could. Any reader looking for allusions to Cold War spy novels undoubtedly would have suspected the emissary from the moment his name was revealed.

Another notable change in this third *Princess the Cat* book is that a person's name is finally revealed. The oldest girl child's name, Sarah, had to be revealed during dialogue and wasn't easily avoidable. Of course, for Princess, humans are minor actors who don't really deserve to be named in her adventures. And lastly, I, the middle boy child, never owned a BB gun, and I certainly never shot at a dog, let alone kill one!

Also, I'm not sure how much a tropical bird like a parrot would be flying around in the freezing cold. I'm certain a real parrot couldn't survive long in such conditions. However, the animals in my stories do many impossible things, so I hope the reader can overlook this one as well.

If you enjoyed this adventure, please leave a review. It's a big help to me, and it helps others discover Princess the Cat.

Lastly, if you haven't already, join the Flannel and Flashlight Newsletter, and you will definitely get something worthwhile, but I can't promise what that is when you will be reading this. It will probably be short story or something like that. Sign up at this link, http://bit.ly/FandFNewsletter

Awesome,

John Heaton

June, 2017

Princess the Cat Defeats the Emperor

A Cat and Dog Children's Book Christmas Caper

Copyright 2017 - John Heaton
     All rights reserved.

Flannel and Flashlight Press
     Cissna Park, IL

www.flannelandflashlight.com

First Print Edition
     ISBN: 9781549647178

56476705R00086

Made in the USA
San Bernardino, CA
11 November 2017